MARVEL
THE AVENGERS
BEGINNINGS

written by **THOMAS MACRI**
illustrated by **LUKE ROSS & DEAN WHITE**

LOS ANGELES / NEW YORK

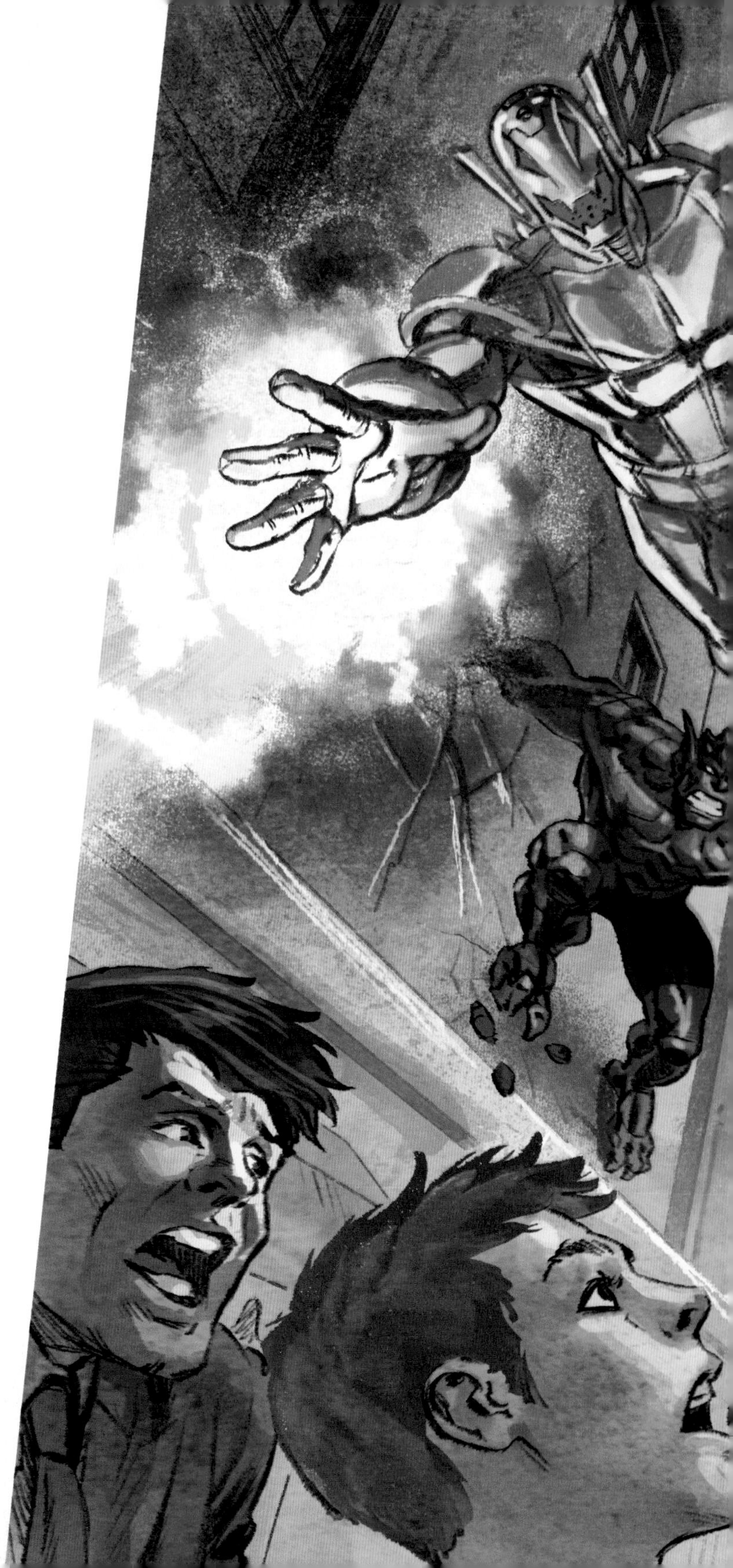

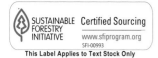

Printed in the
United States of America
First Edition, April 2015
10 9 8 7 6 5 4 3 2 1
G942-9090-6-15051
ISBN 978-1-4847-1382-2
Library of Congress Control Number:
2014944505

For information address Marvel Press, 125 West End Avenue, New York, New York 10023.

Designed by Jennifer Redding and John J. Hill.

MARVEL

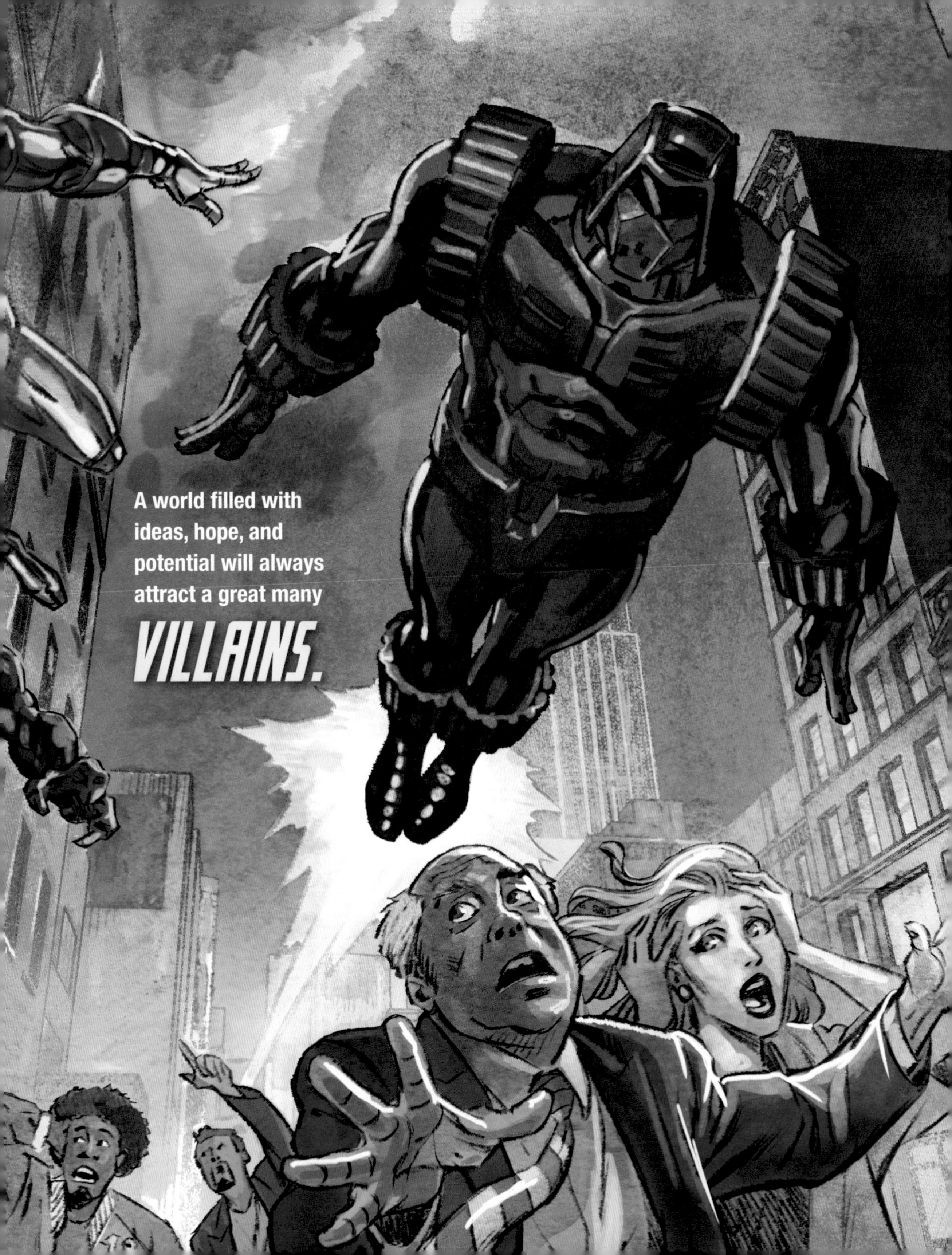
A world filled with ideas, hope, and potential will always attract a great many
VILLAINS.

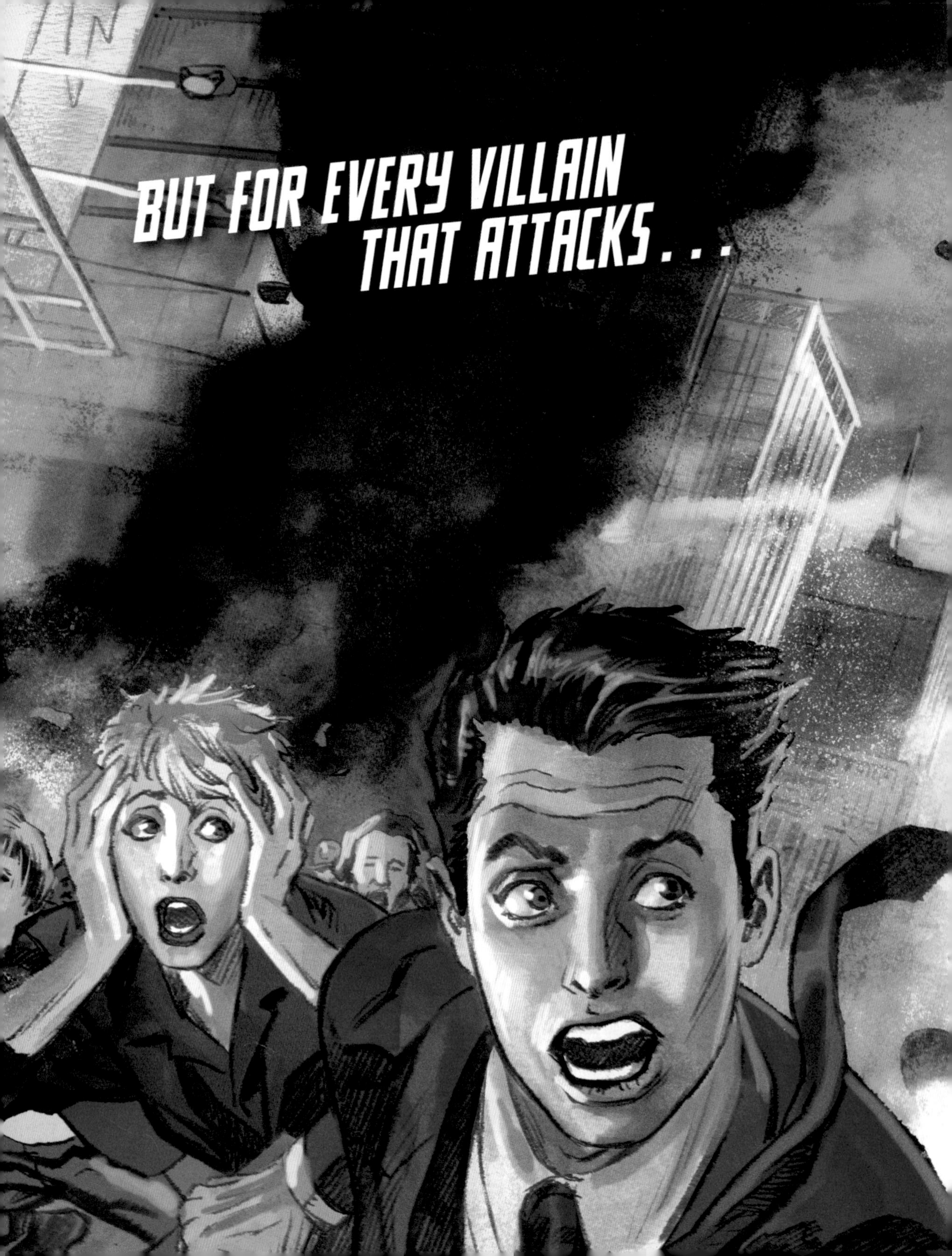
BUT FOR EVERY VILLAIN THAT ATTACKS . . .

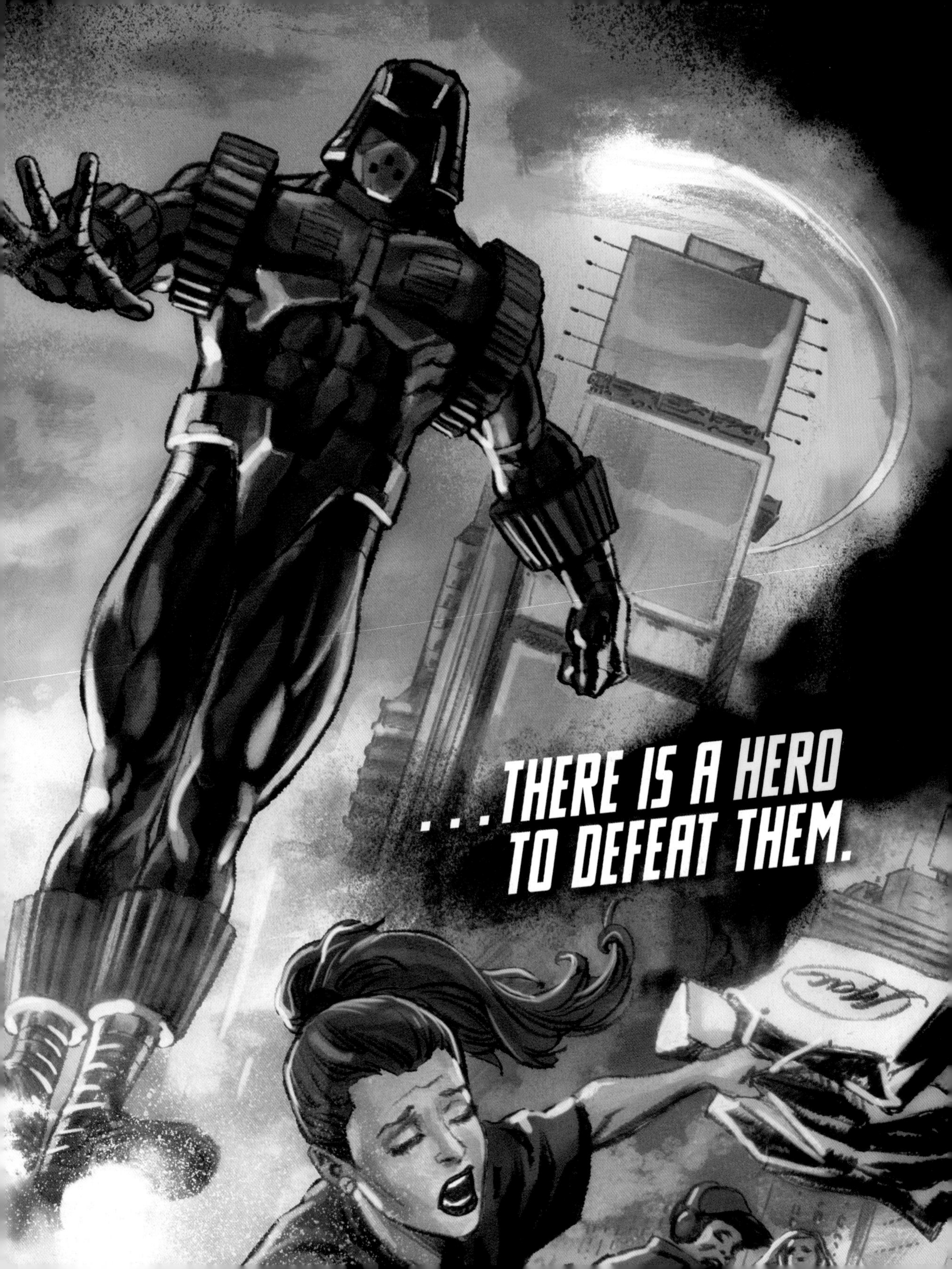
. . . THERE IS A HERO
TO DEFEAT THEM.

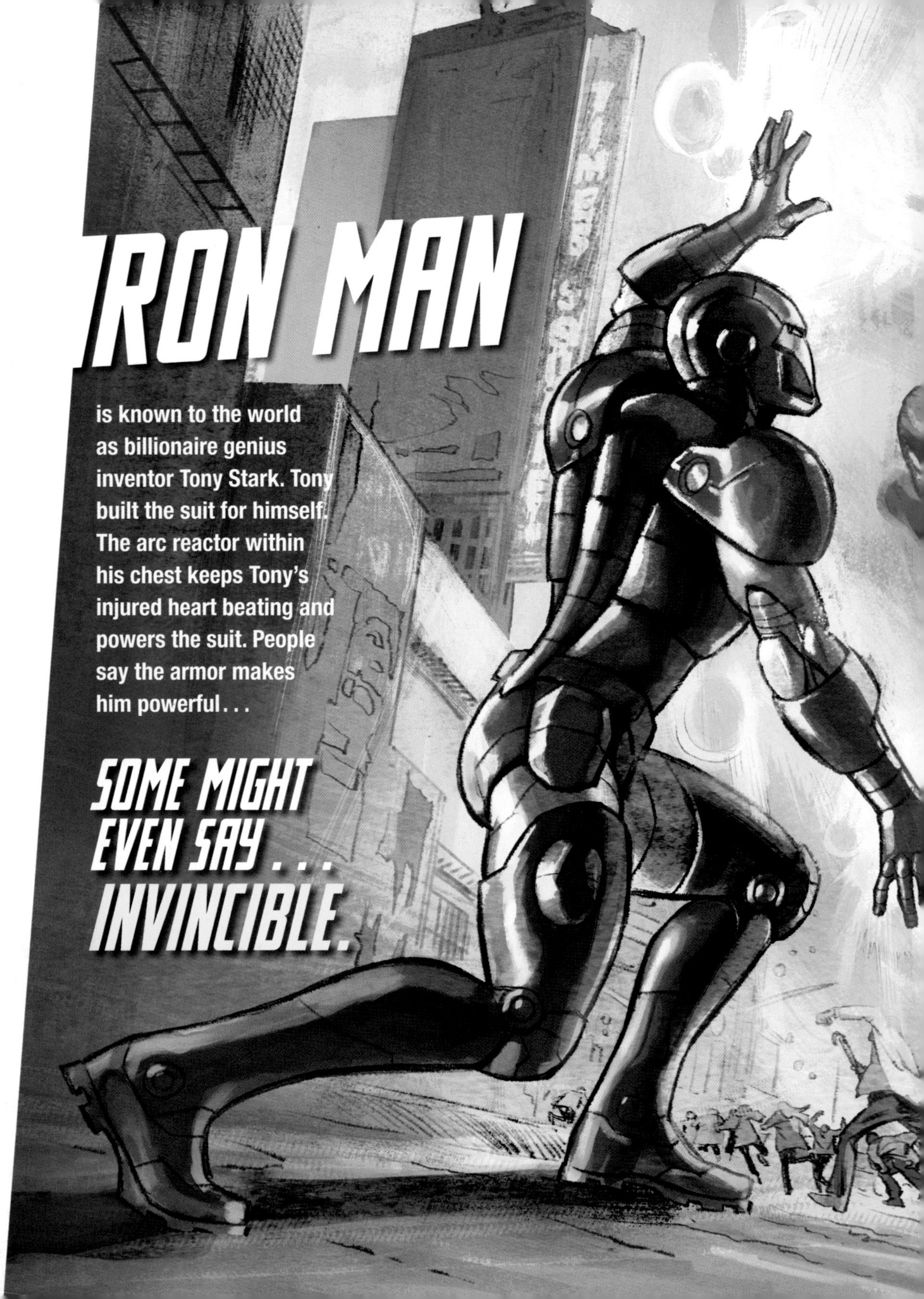

IRON MAN

is known to the world as billionaire genius inventor Tony Stark. Tony built the suit for himself. The arc reactor within his chest keeps Tony's injured heart beating and powers the suit. People say the armor makes him powerful . . .

SOME MIGHT EVEN SAY . . . INVINCIBLE.

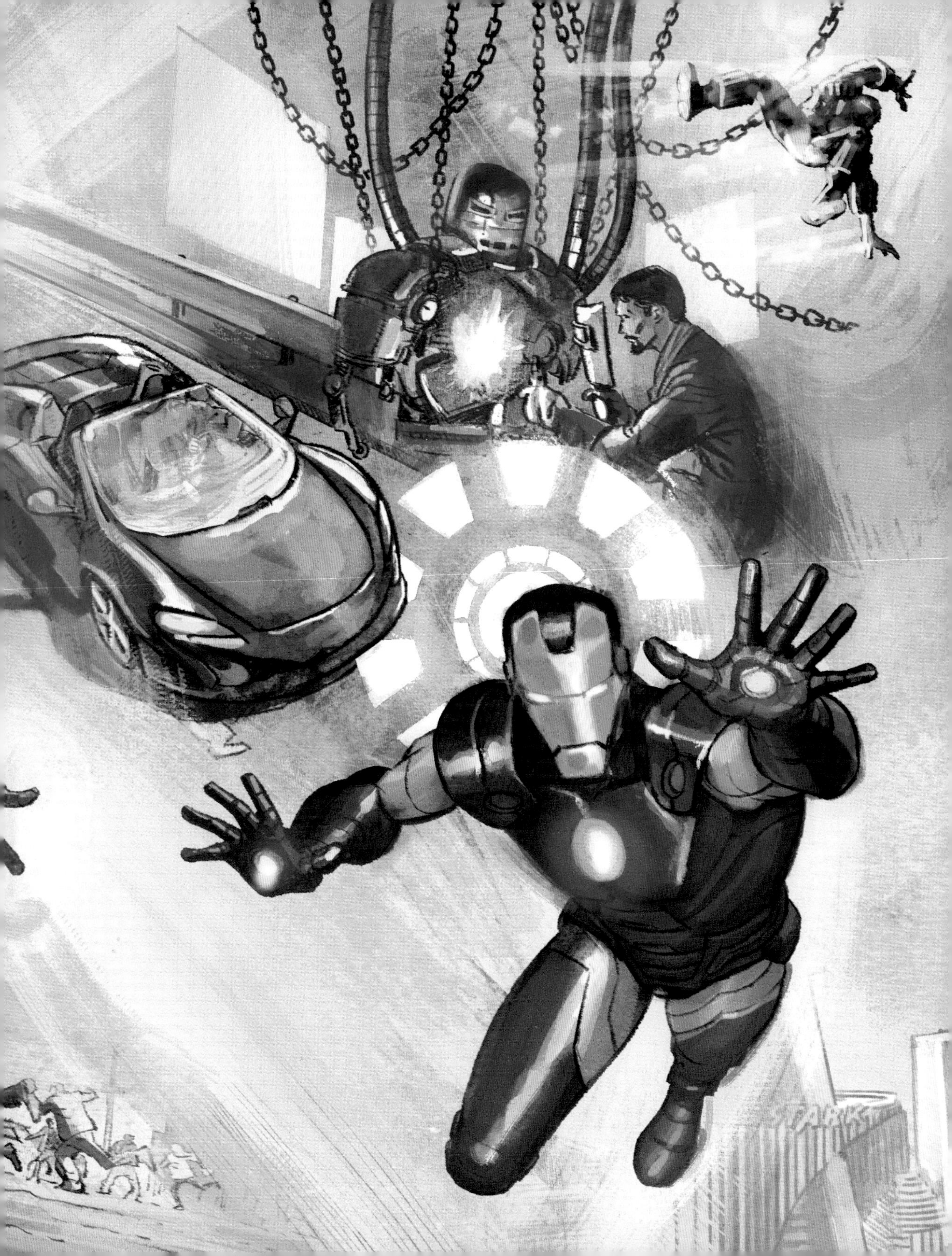
STARK

Tony was not alone. Natasha Romanoff spent years training to be a top secret spy, handling missions some thought to be myth. Eventually, Natasha was recruited by Nick Fury and S.H.I.E.L.D. where she was given high-tech equipment and the codename...

BLACK WIDOW.

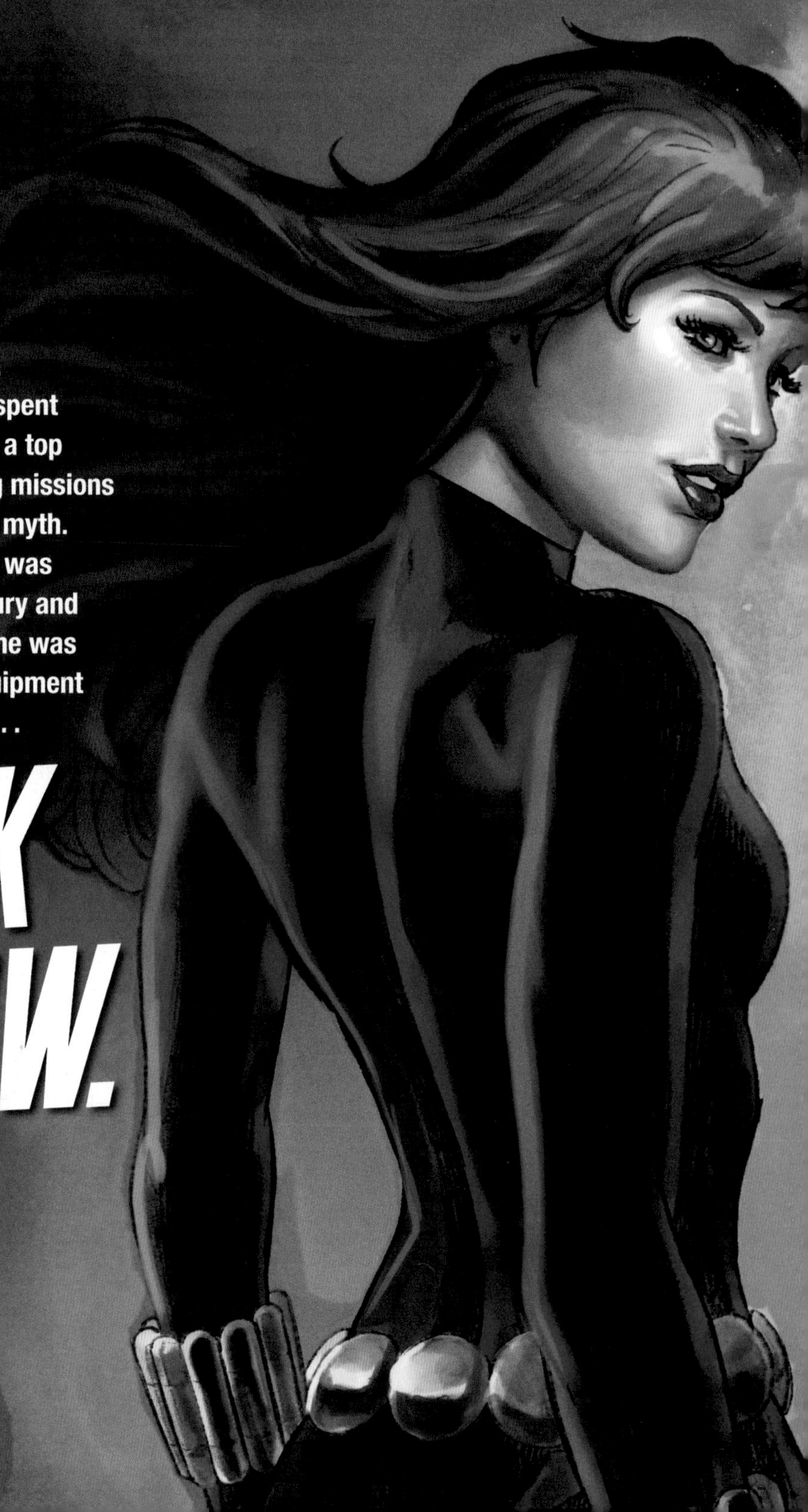

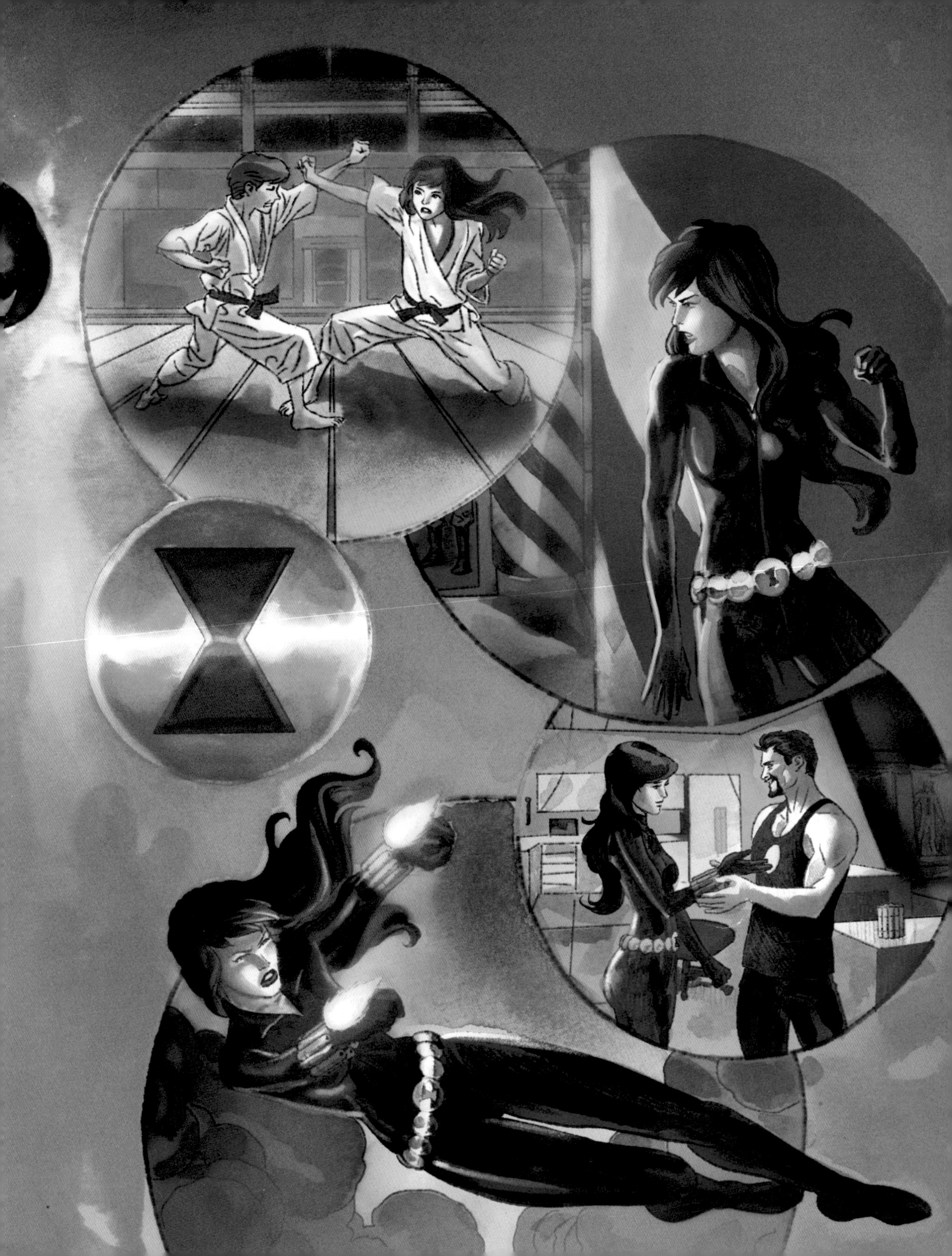

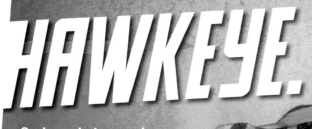

And Black Widow could always rely on

HAWKEYE.

Orphaned at an early age, Clint Barton worked for a traveling circus as a master archer. After witnessing Iron Man rescue people in danger, Clint knew he, too, wanted to be a Super Hero and help those in need. Clint made a costume and created a variety of trick arrows, equipped with exploding tips, stunners, and electrical nets. He became known as Hawkeye and joined the mighty Avengers.

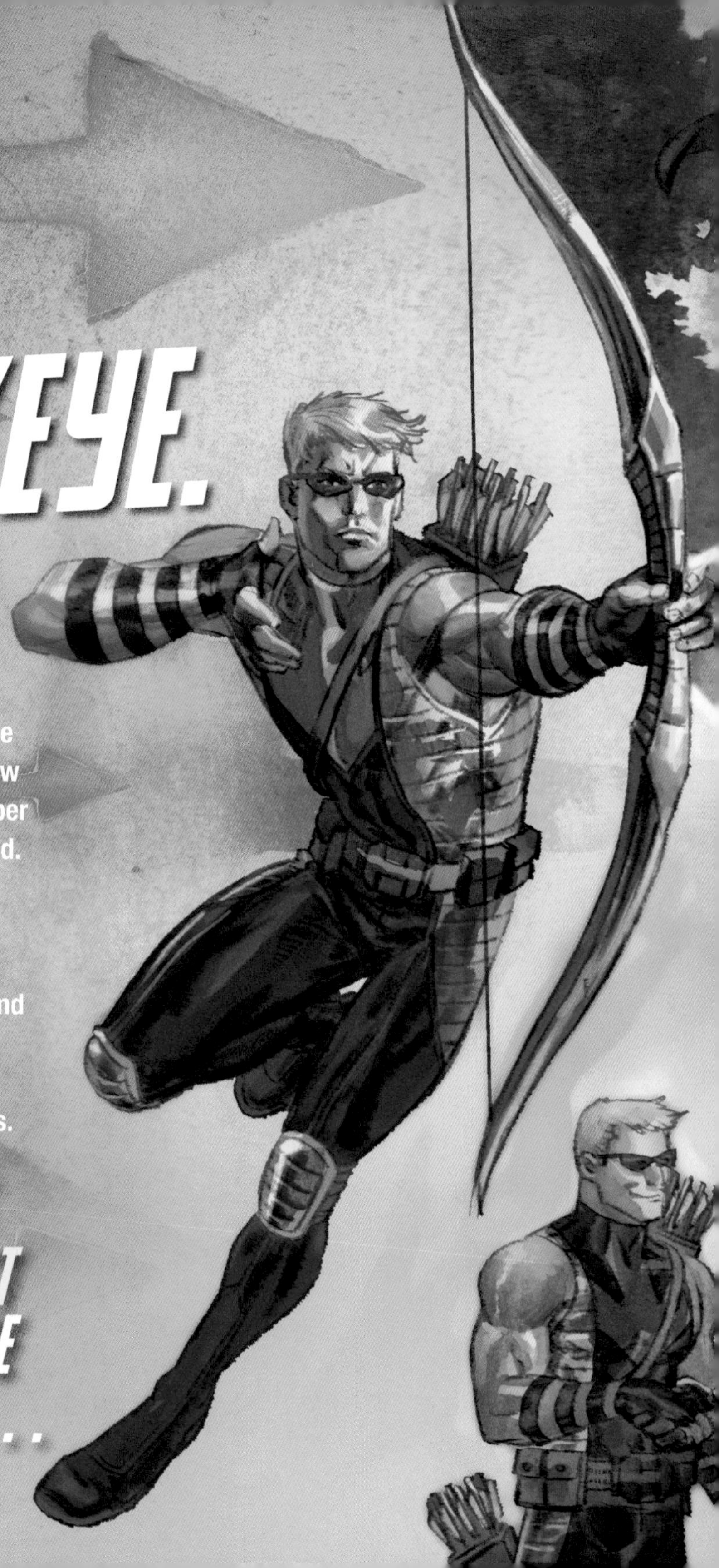

AND WHEN HIS ARROWS DIDN'T CUT IT. . .THERE WAS ALWAYS. . .

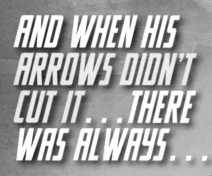

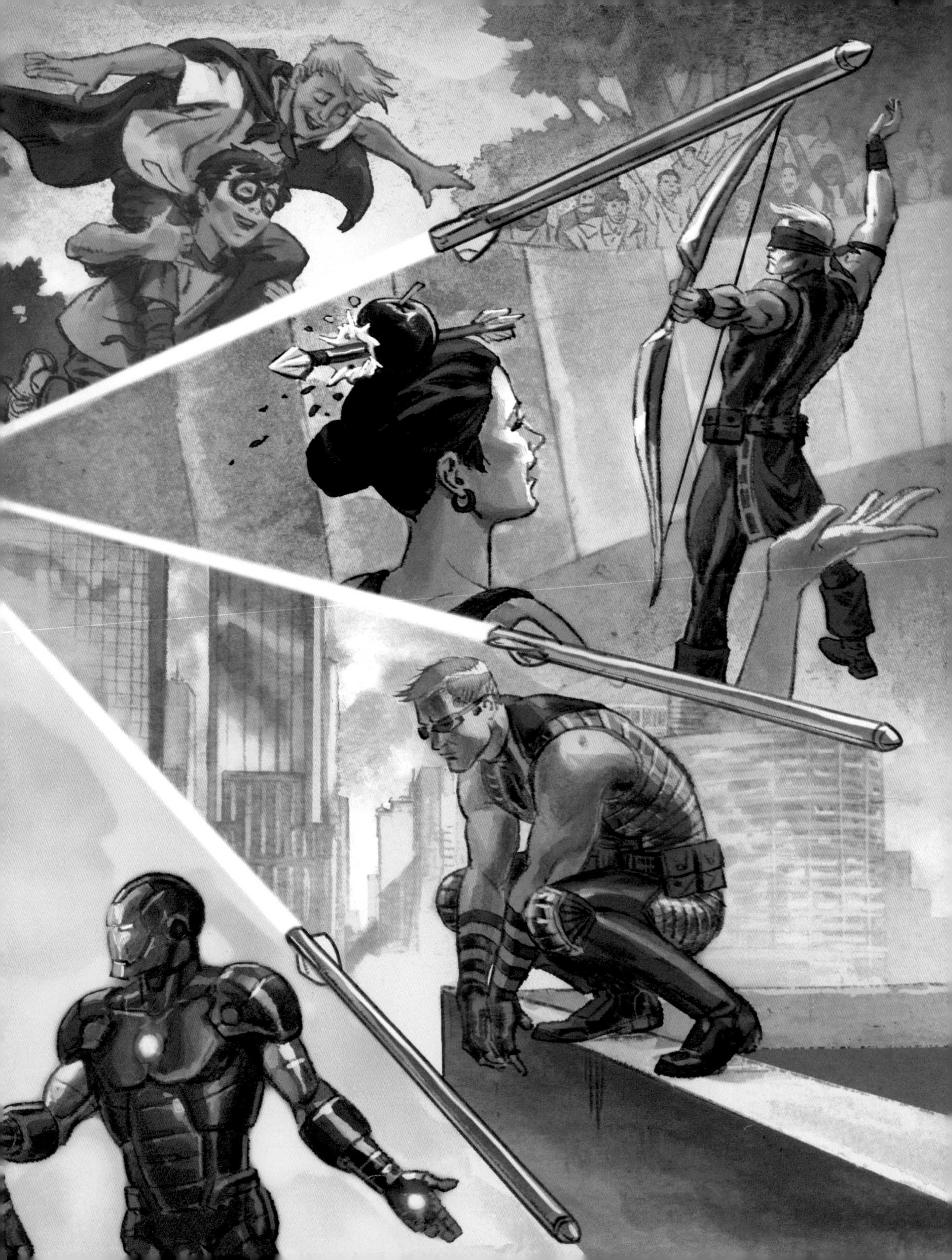

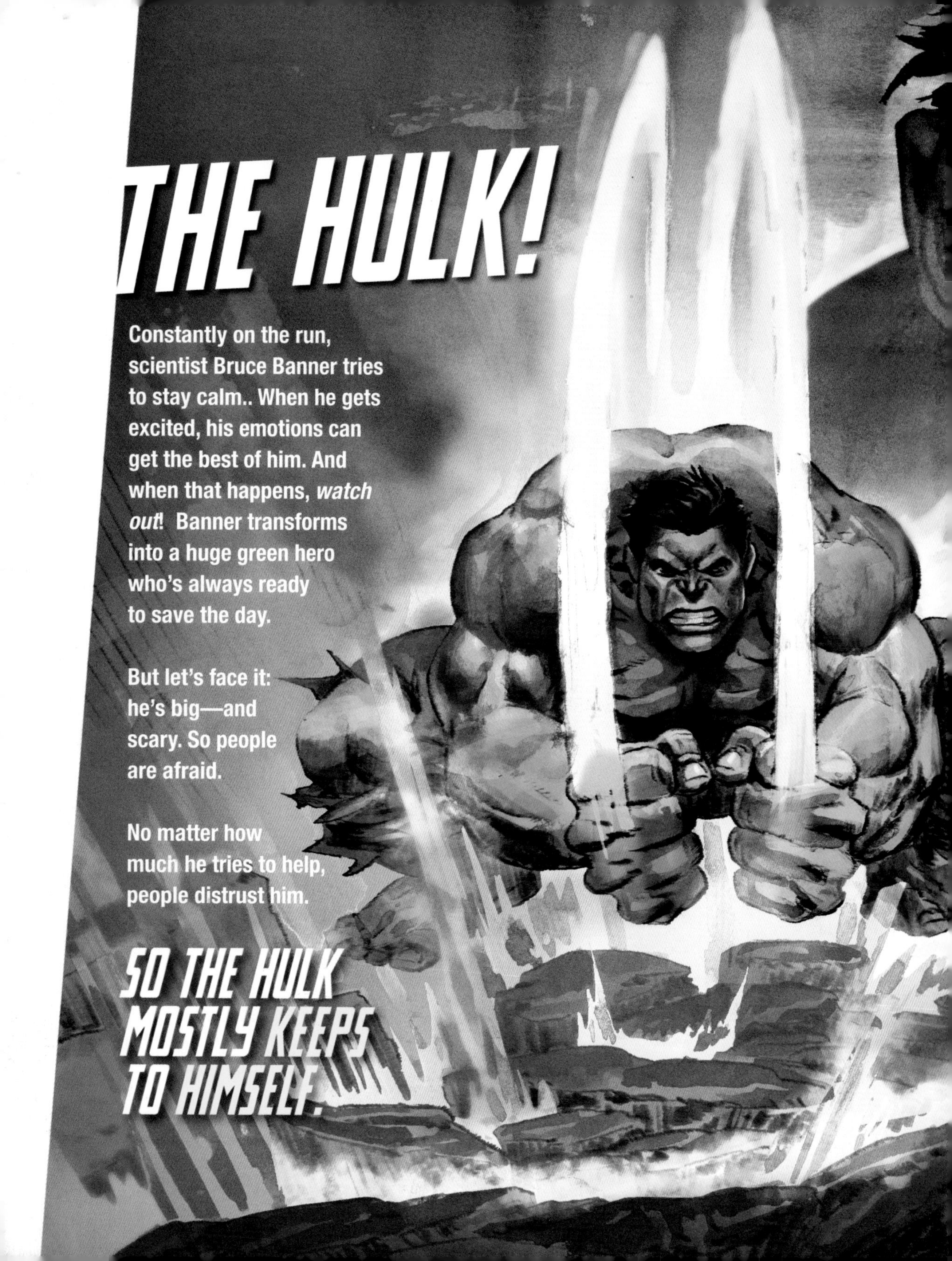

THE HULK!

Constantly on the run, scientist Bruce Banner tries to stay calm.. When he gets excited, his emotions can get the best of him. And when that happens, *watch out*! Banner transforms into a huge green hero who's always ready to save the day.

But let's face it: he's big—and scary. So people are afraid.

No matter how much he tries to help, people distrust him.

SO THE HULK MOSTLY KEEPS TO HIMSELF.

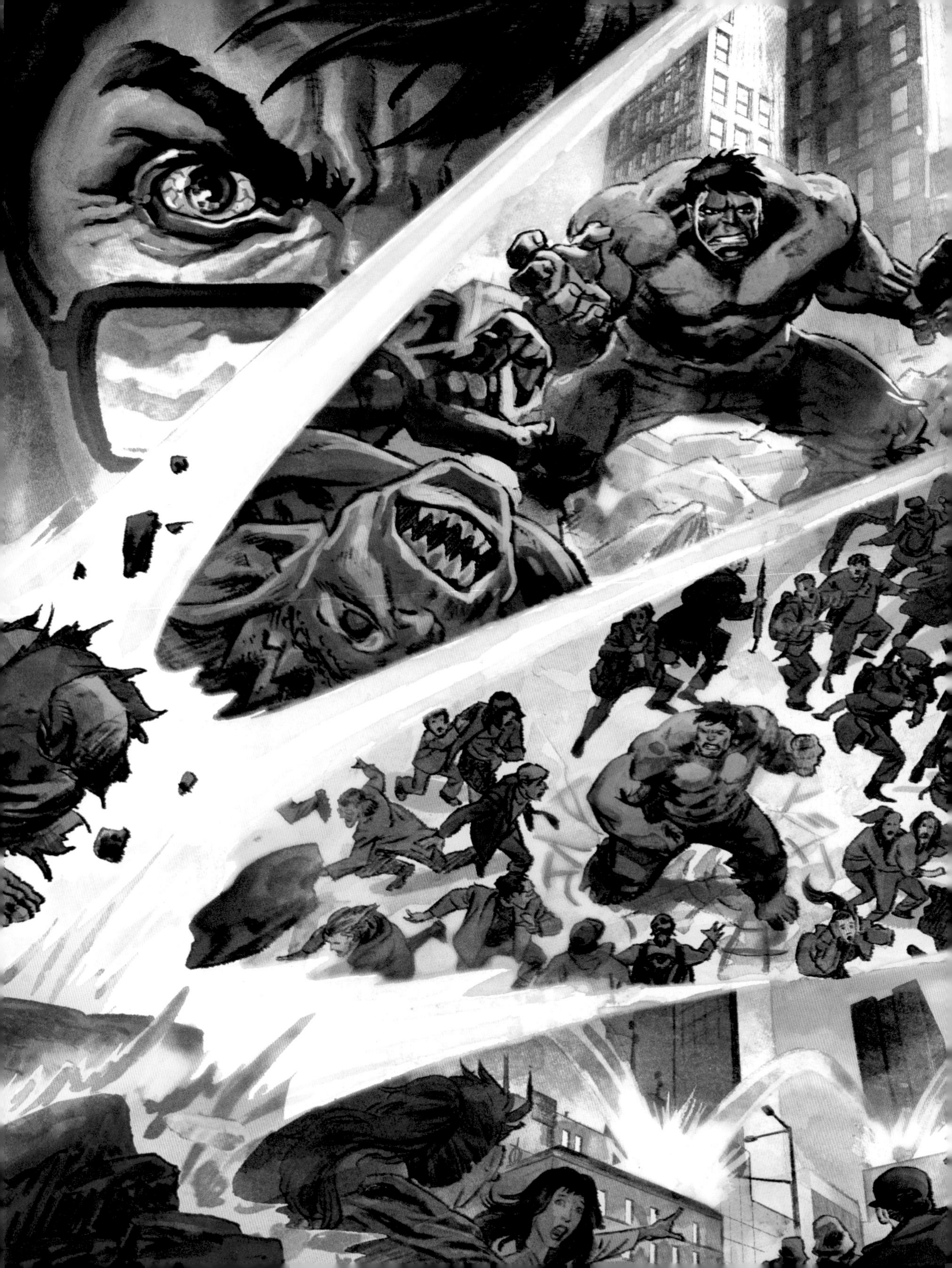

Far away, in a place called Asgard,

THOR

made someone very angry. His brother, Loki, wanted to rule Asgard—or anywhere else, for that matter. So Thor imprisoned his brother on a place called the Isle of Silence.

Loki didn't take this well at all. He wanted revenge!

Loki used his powers to search the Earth—a place his brother loves and has sworn to protect—to find someone people feared. Someone they distrusted...

BUT, ABOVE ALL, SOMEONE WHO COULD DEFEAT HIS BROTHER, THOR.

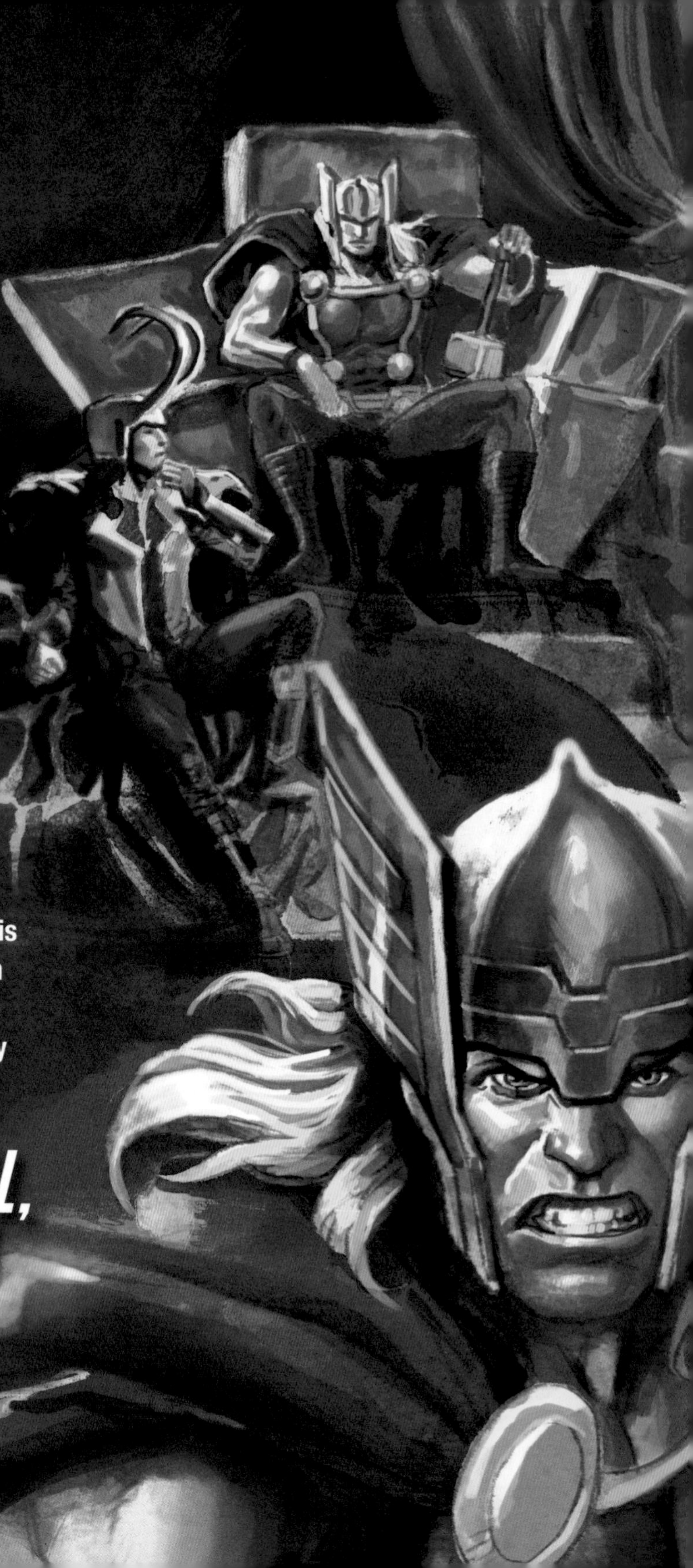

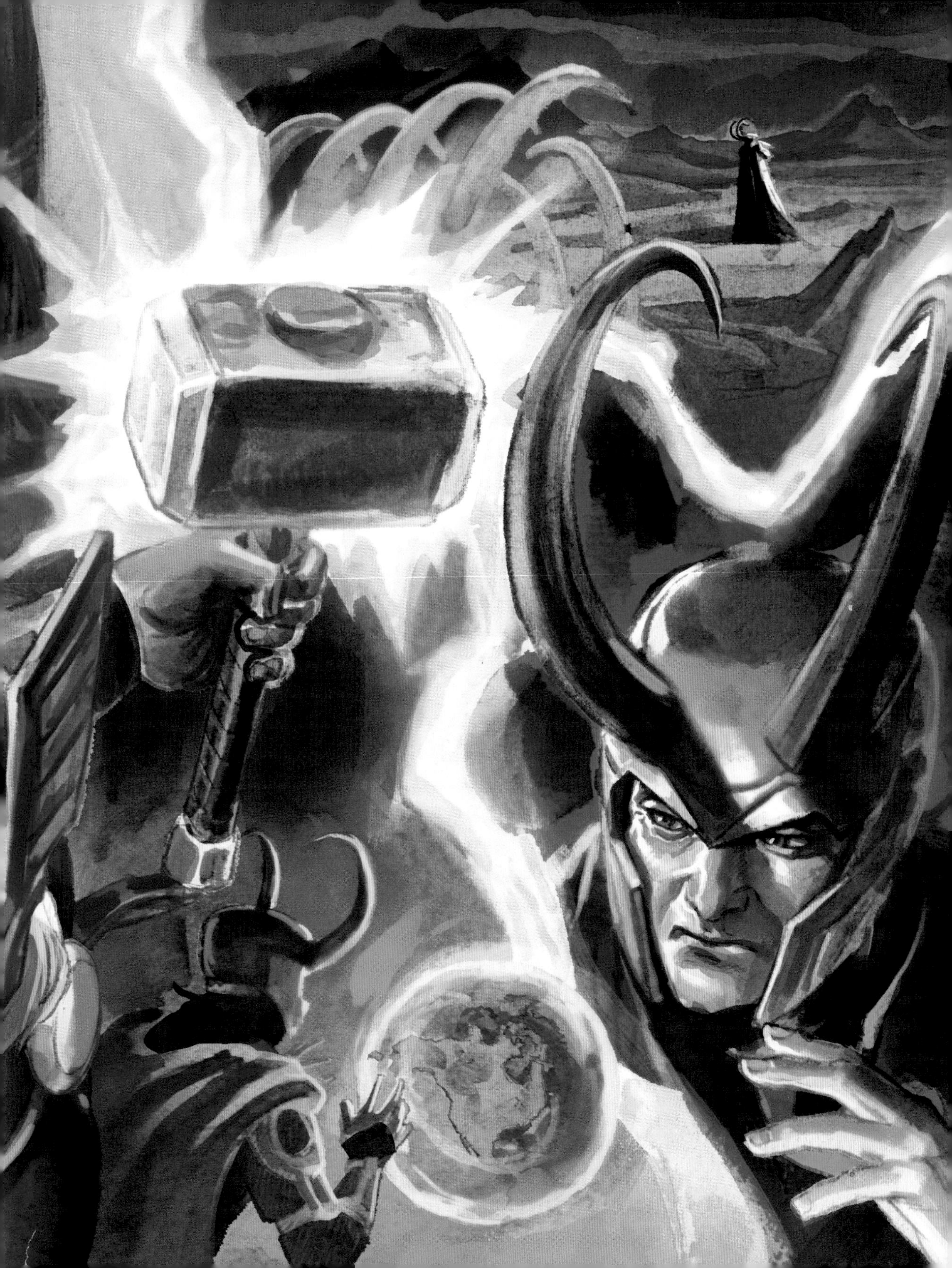

He soon found someone—
the Incredible Hulk!

The master of mischief,

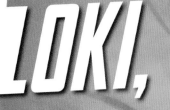

LOKI,

used his powers to trick
the Hulk into thinking a
high-speed train was about
to crash on a broken rail.

The Hulk stopped the
train, thinking he had
saved the day.

But the broken rail was
just an illusion. The people
on the train thought the Hulk
was trying to hurt them.

Word spread fast—

THE HULK WAS ON A RAMPAGE!

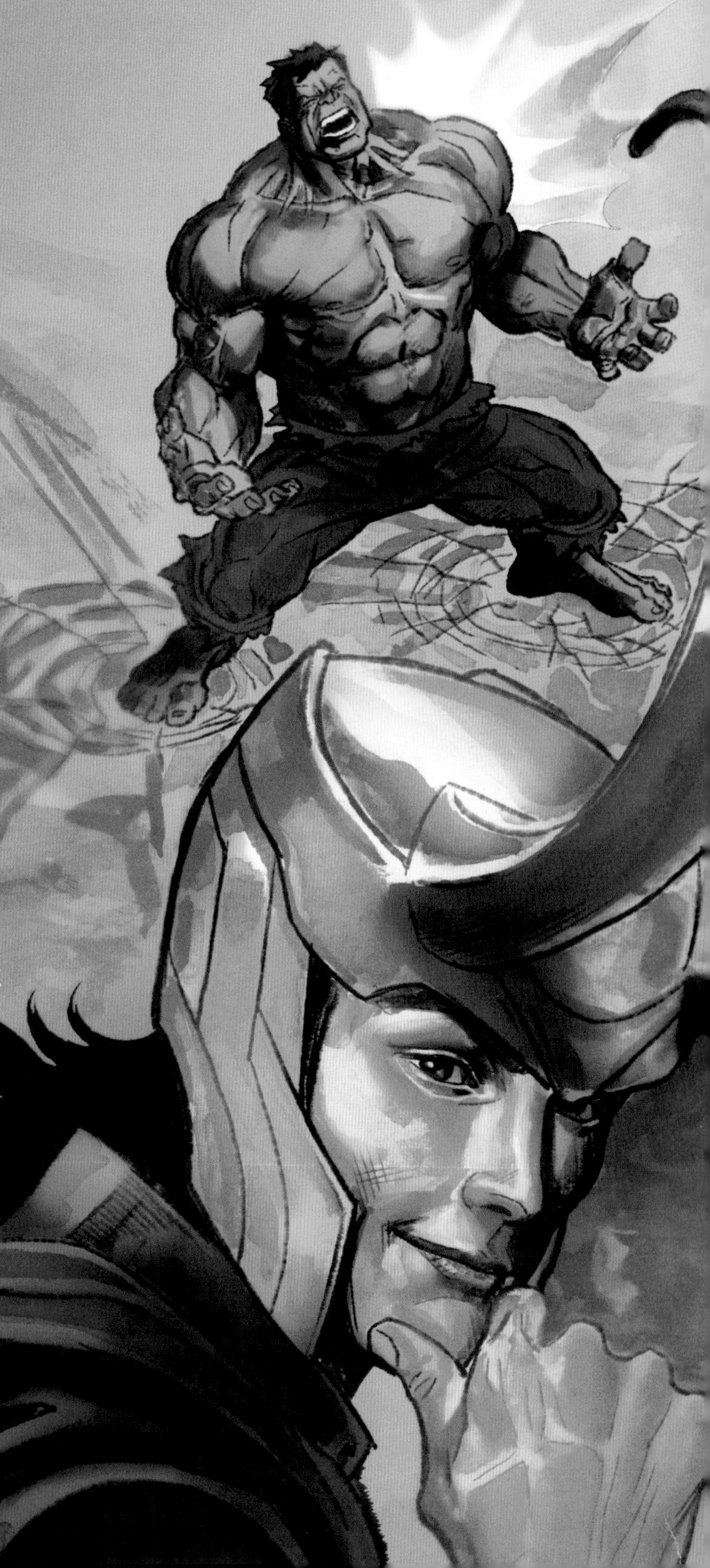

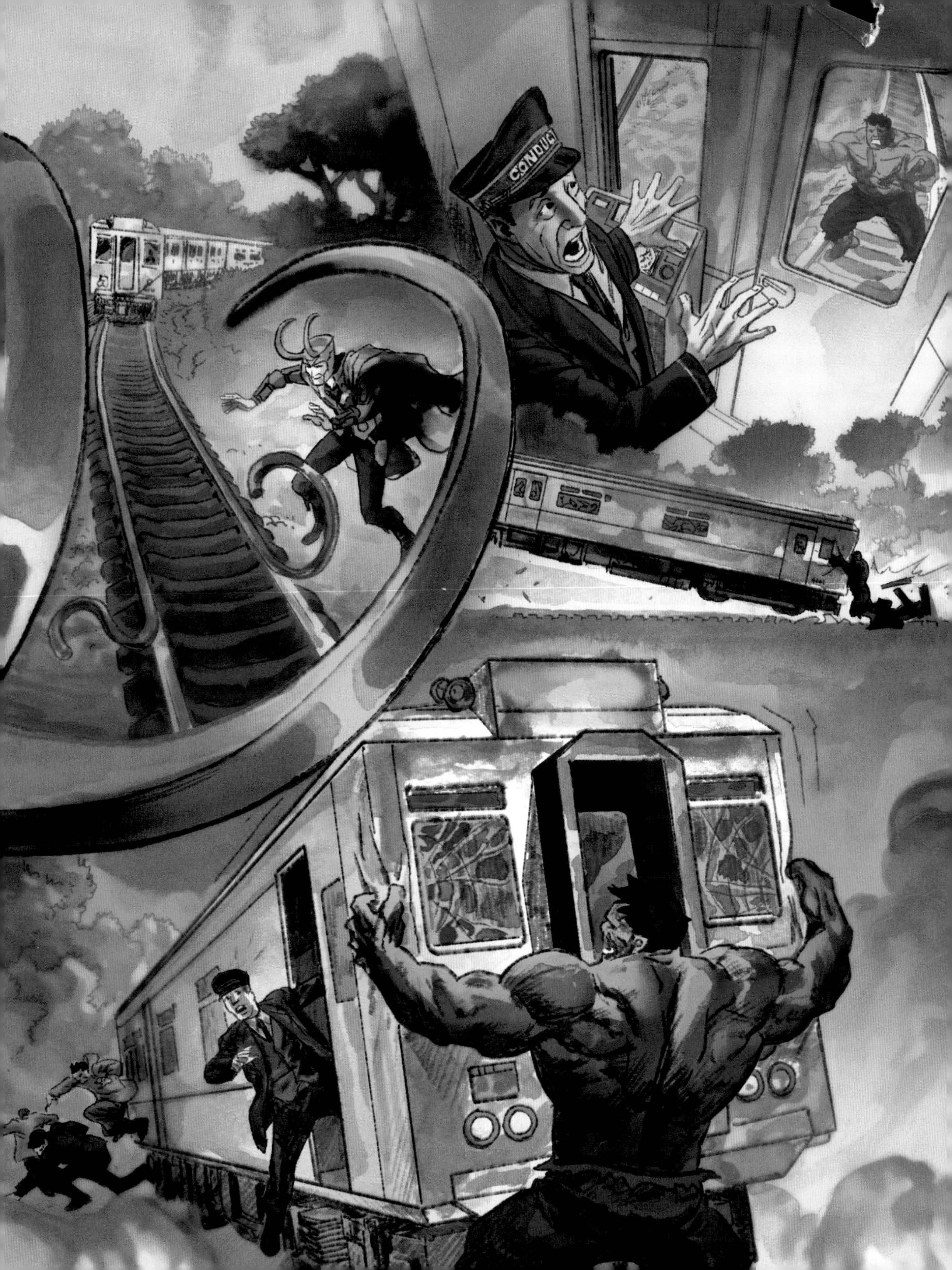

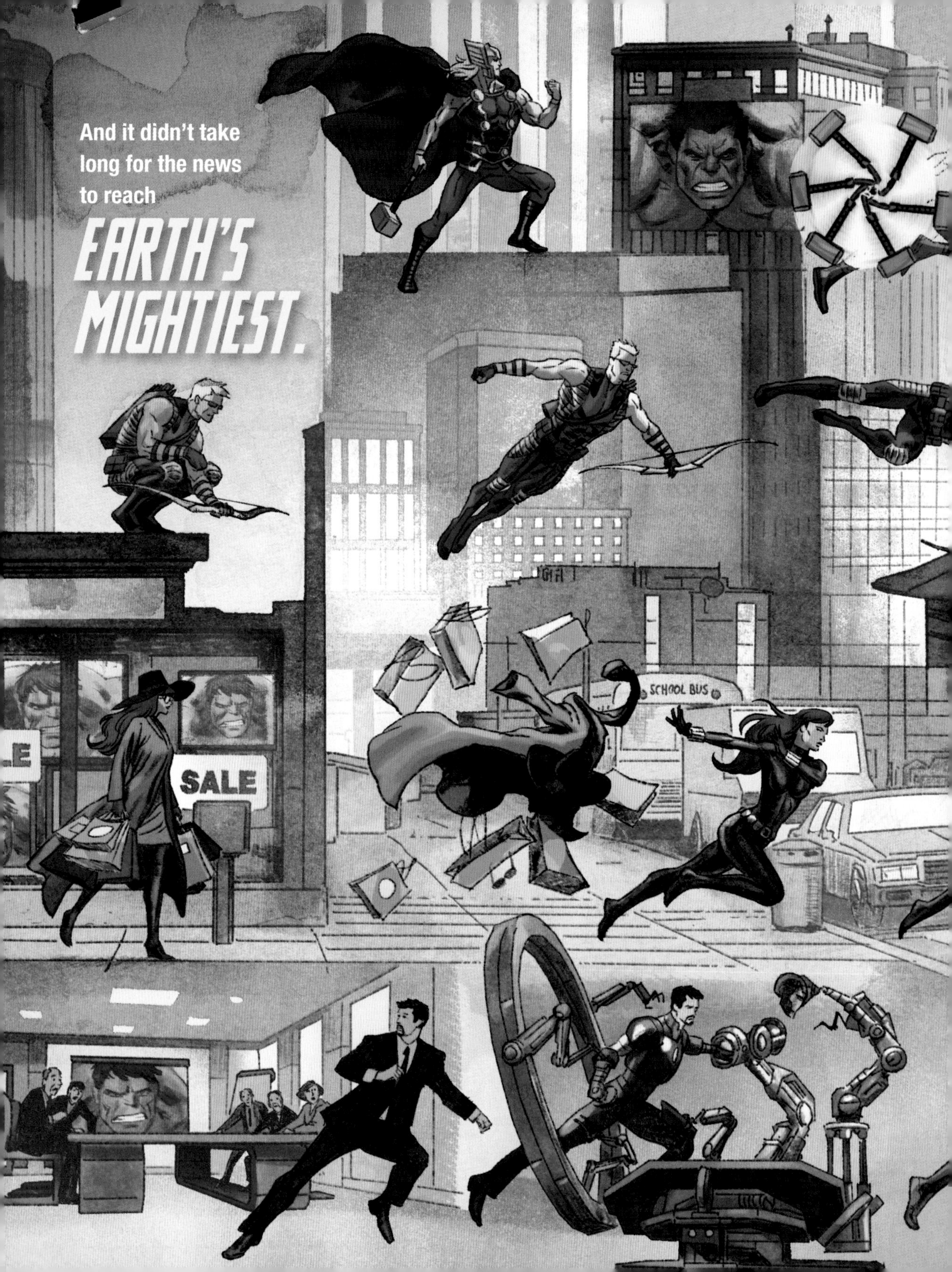
And it didn't take long for the news to reach
EARTH'S MIGHTIEST.
SALE
SCHOOL BUS

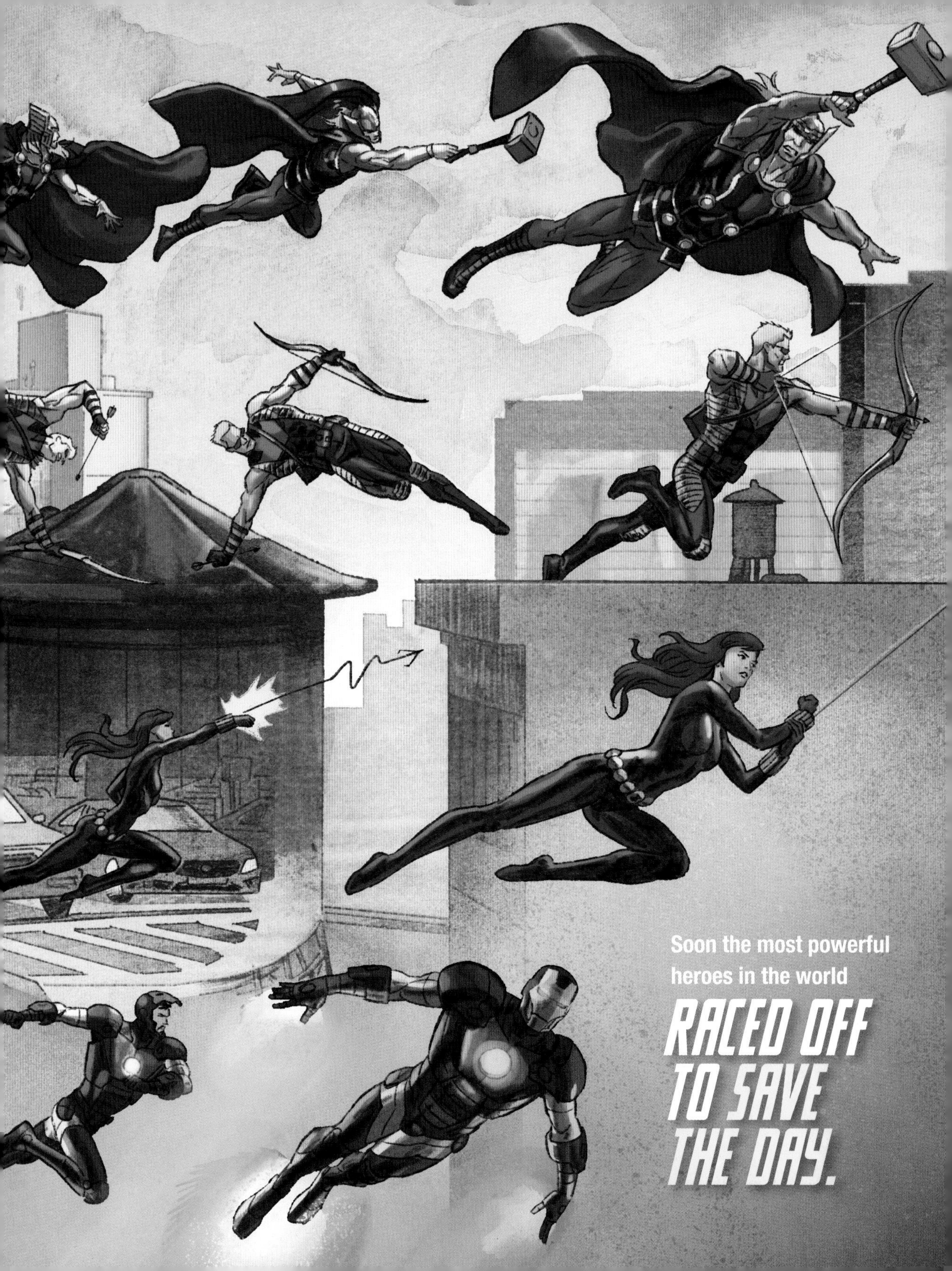

Soon the most powerful heroes in the world

RACED OFF TO SAVE THE DAY.

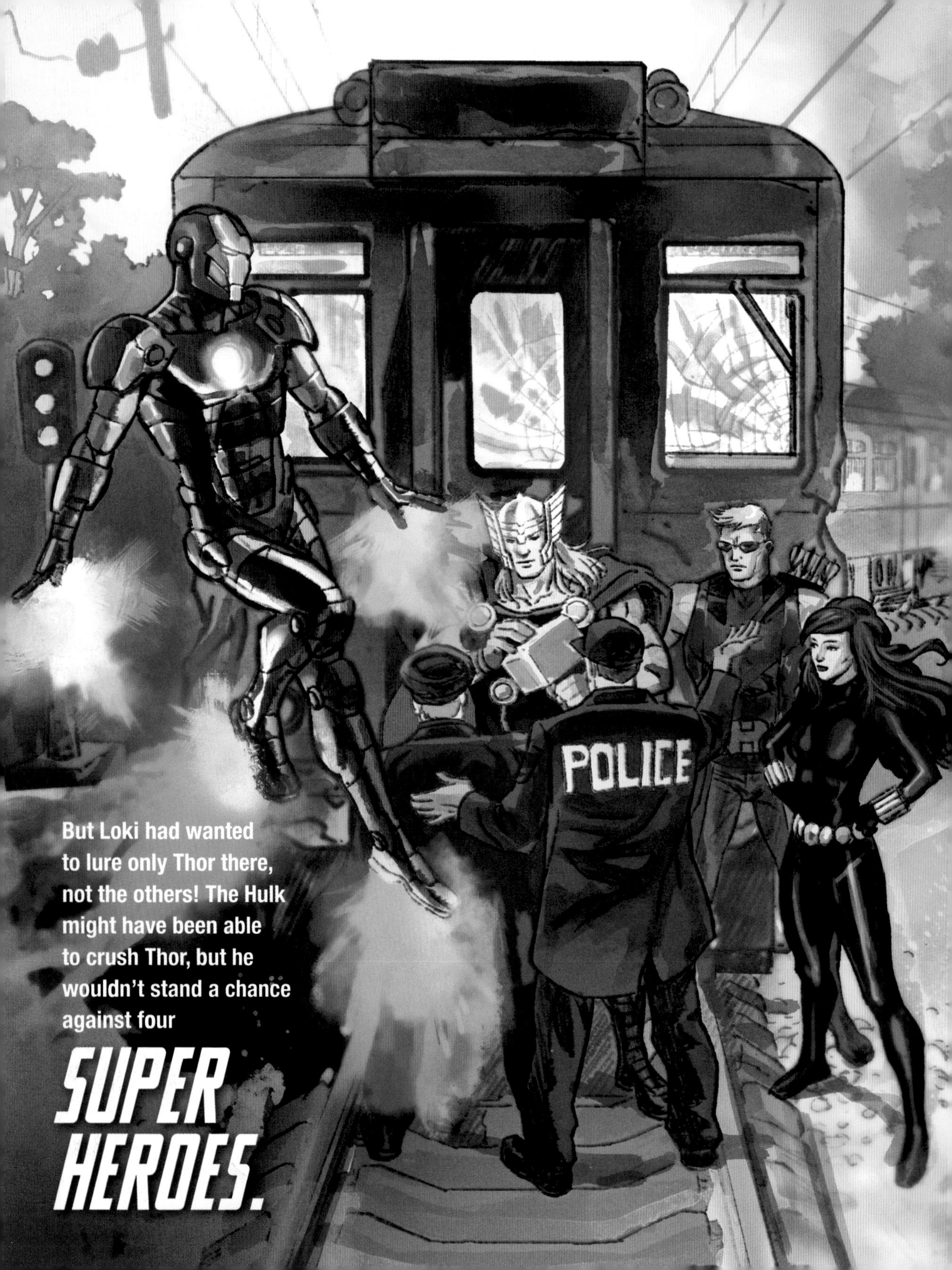
POLICE

But Loki had wanted to lure only Thor there, not the others! The Hulk might have been able to crush Thor, but he wouldn't stand a chance against four

SUPER HEROES.

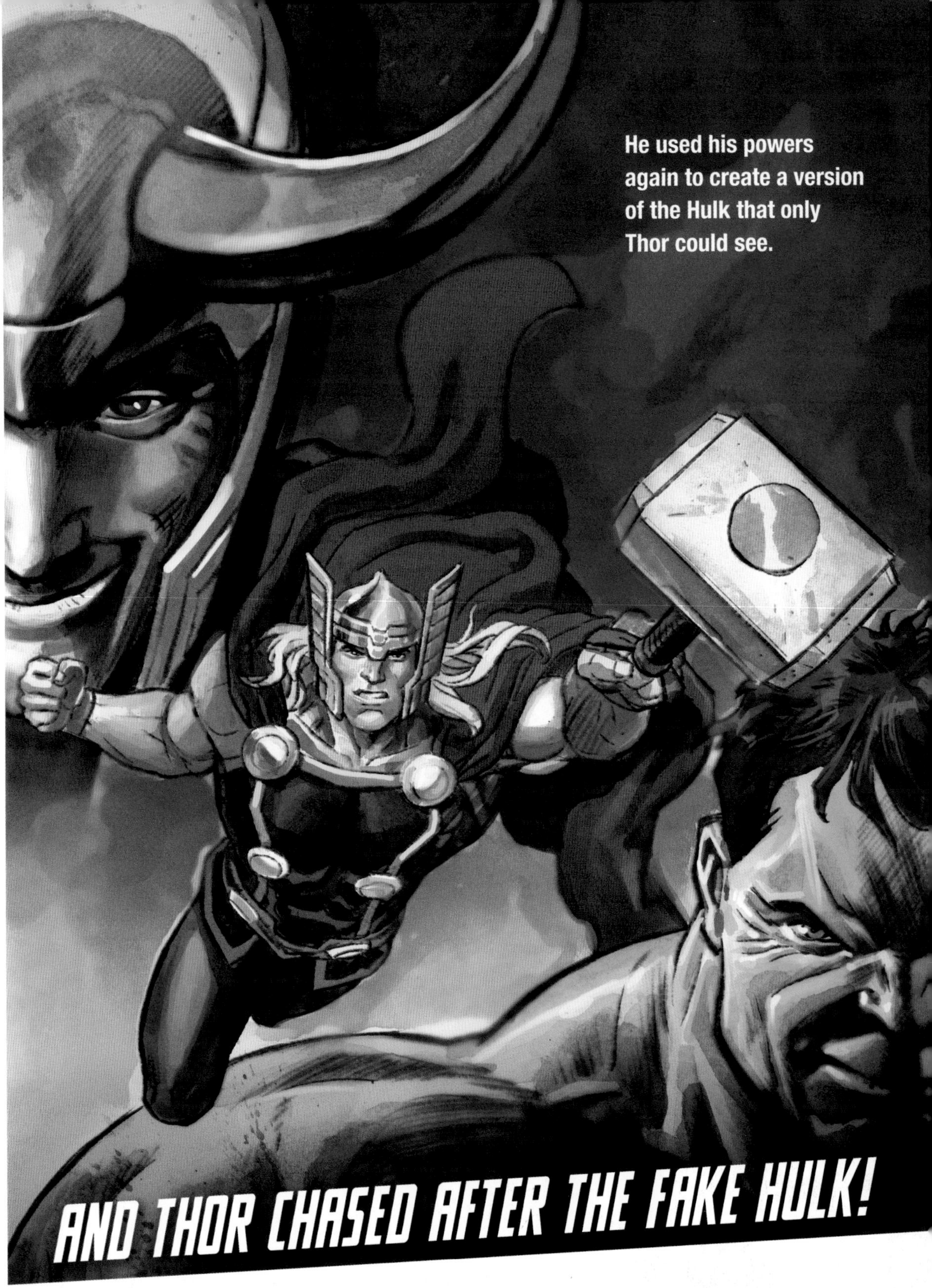

He used his powers again to create a version of the Hulk that only Thor could see.

AND THOR CHASED AFTER THE FAKE HULK!

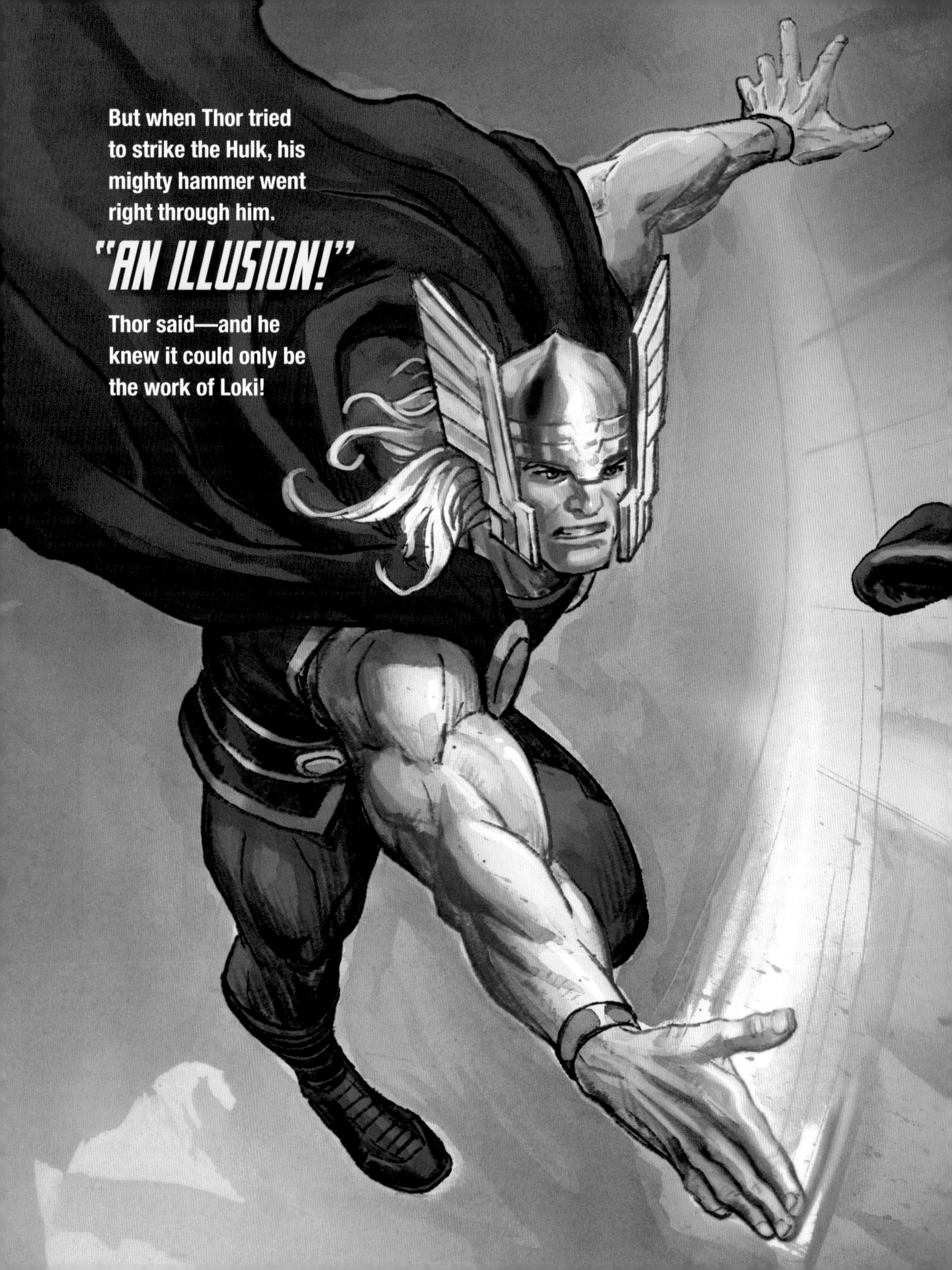

But when Thor tried to strike the Hulk, his mighty hammer went right through him.

"AN ILLUSION!"

Thor said—and he knew it could only be the work of Loki!

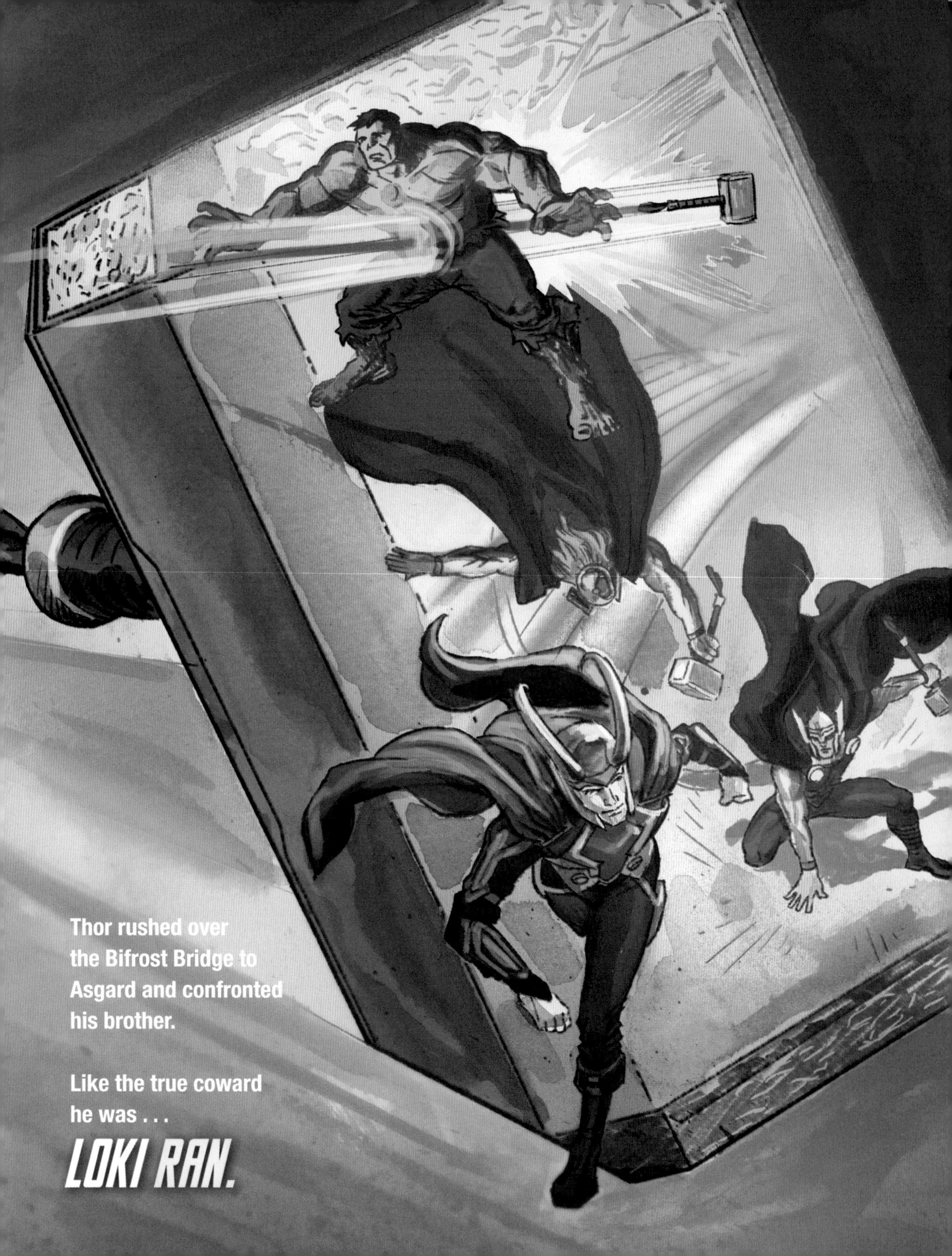

Thor rushed over the Bifrost Bridge to Asgard and confronted his brother.

Like the true coward he was . . .

LOKI RAN.

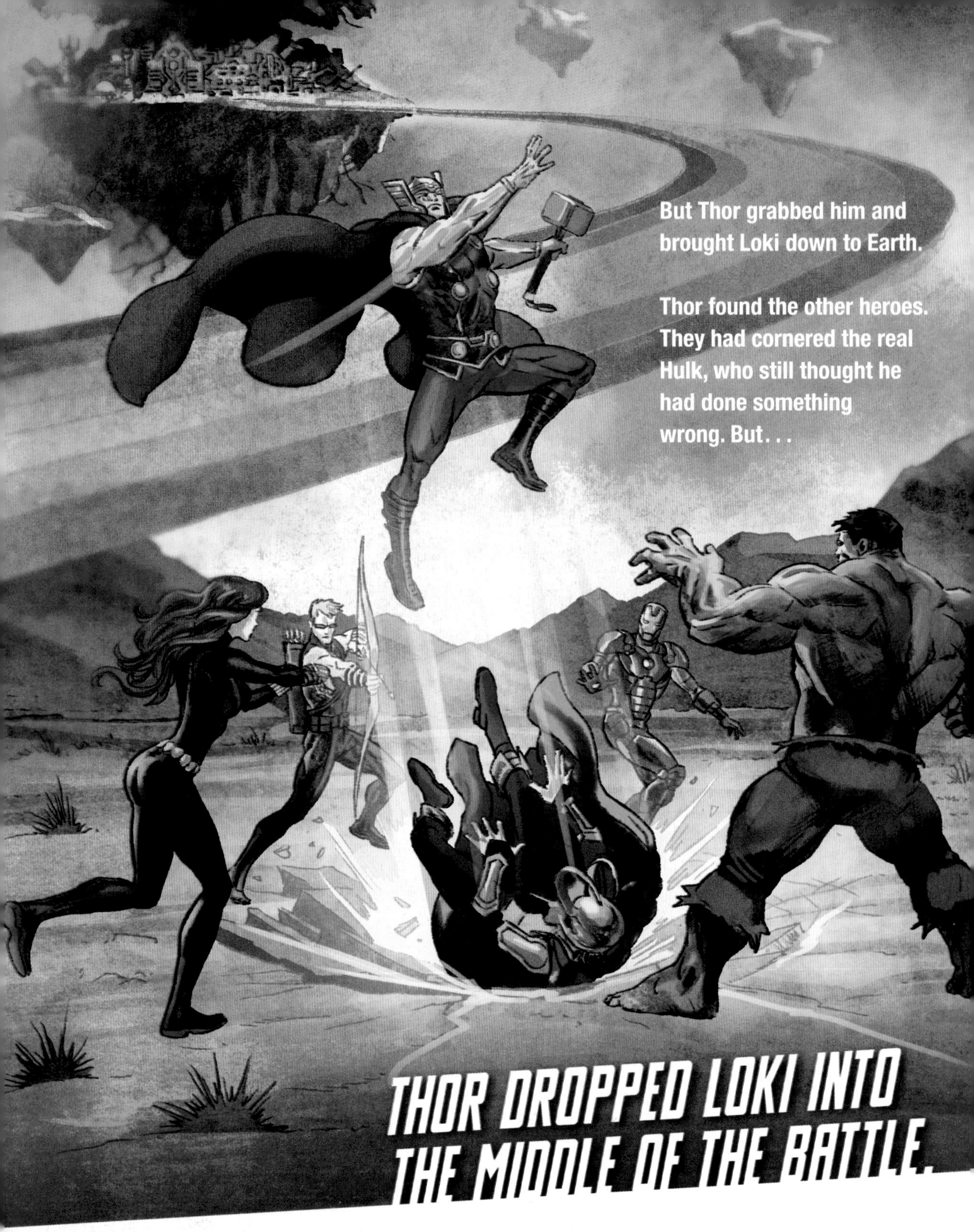

But Thor grabbed him and brought Loki down to Earth.

Thor found the other heroes. They had cornered the real Hulk, who still thought he had done something wrong. But. . .

THOR DROPPED LOKI INTO THE MIDDLE OF THE BATTLE.

"Thou must know—here be your true villain! My brother, Loki of Asgard, tricked thee into believing our comrade, the Hulk, smashed the train!"

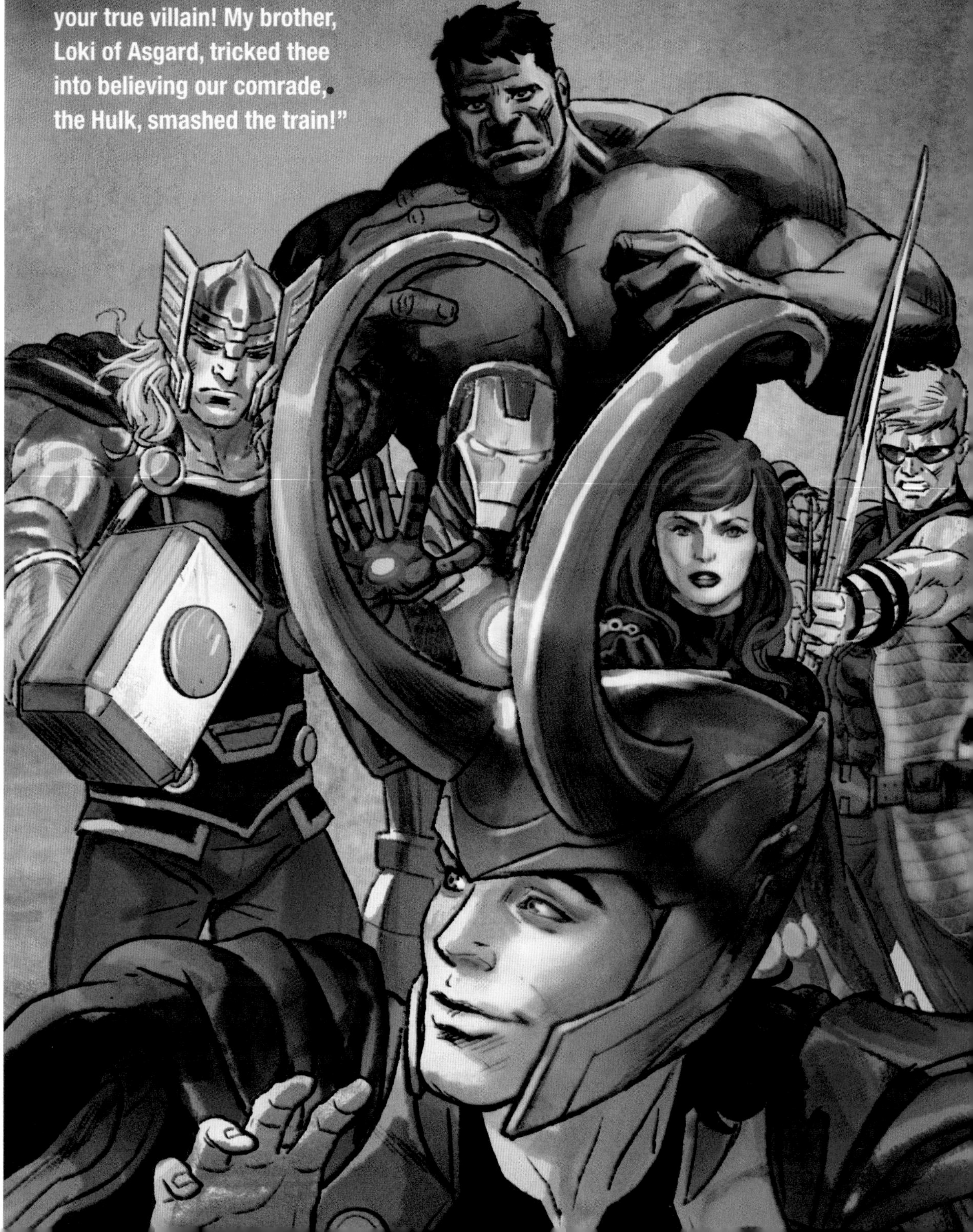

And with that,
Loki used his magic
against the heroes.

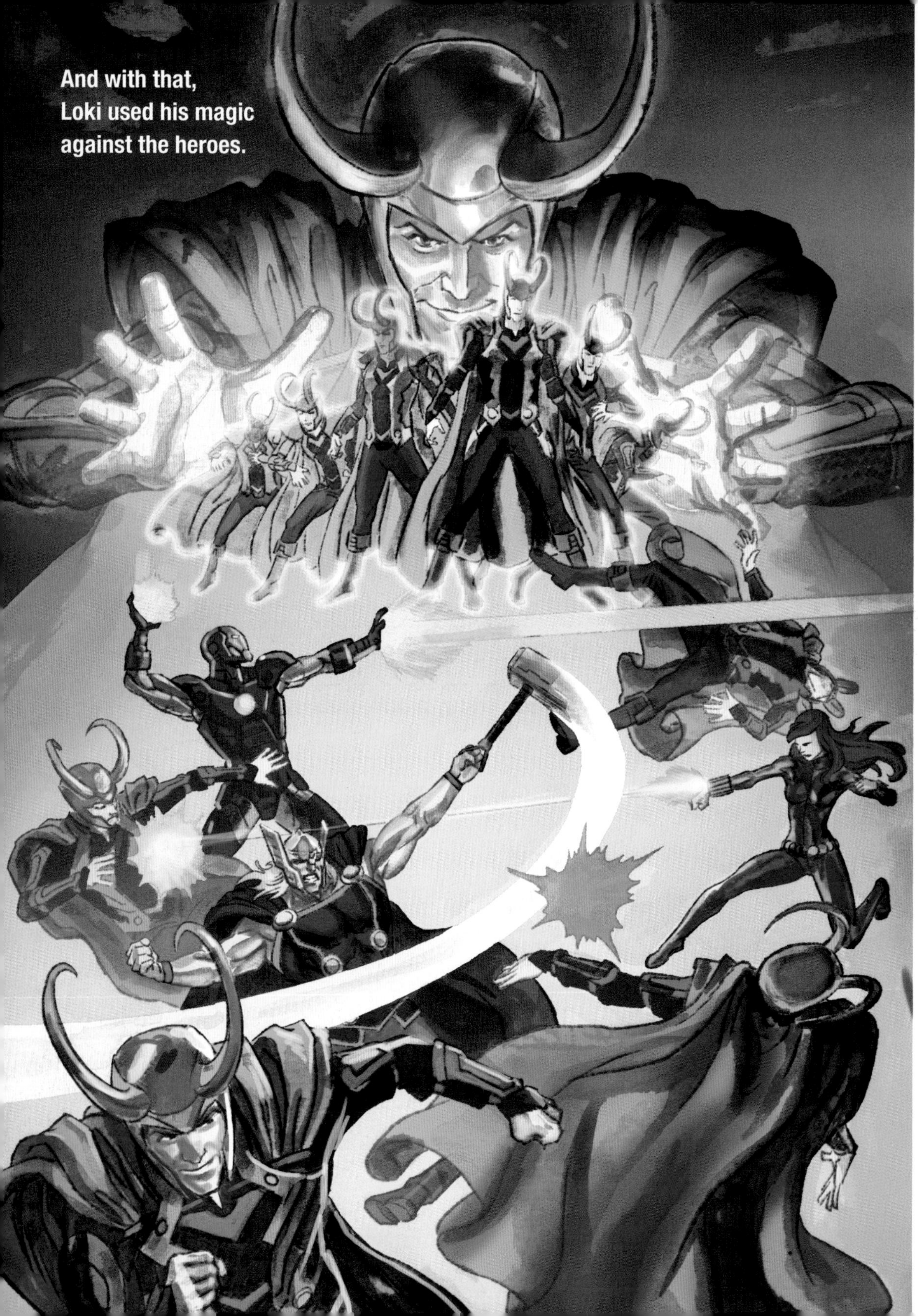

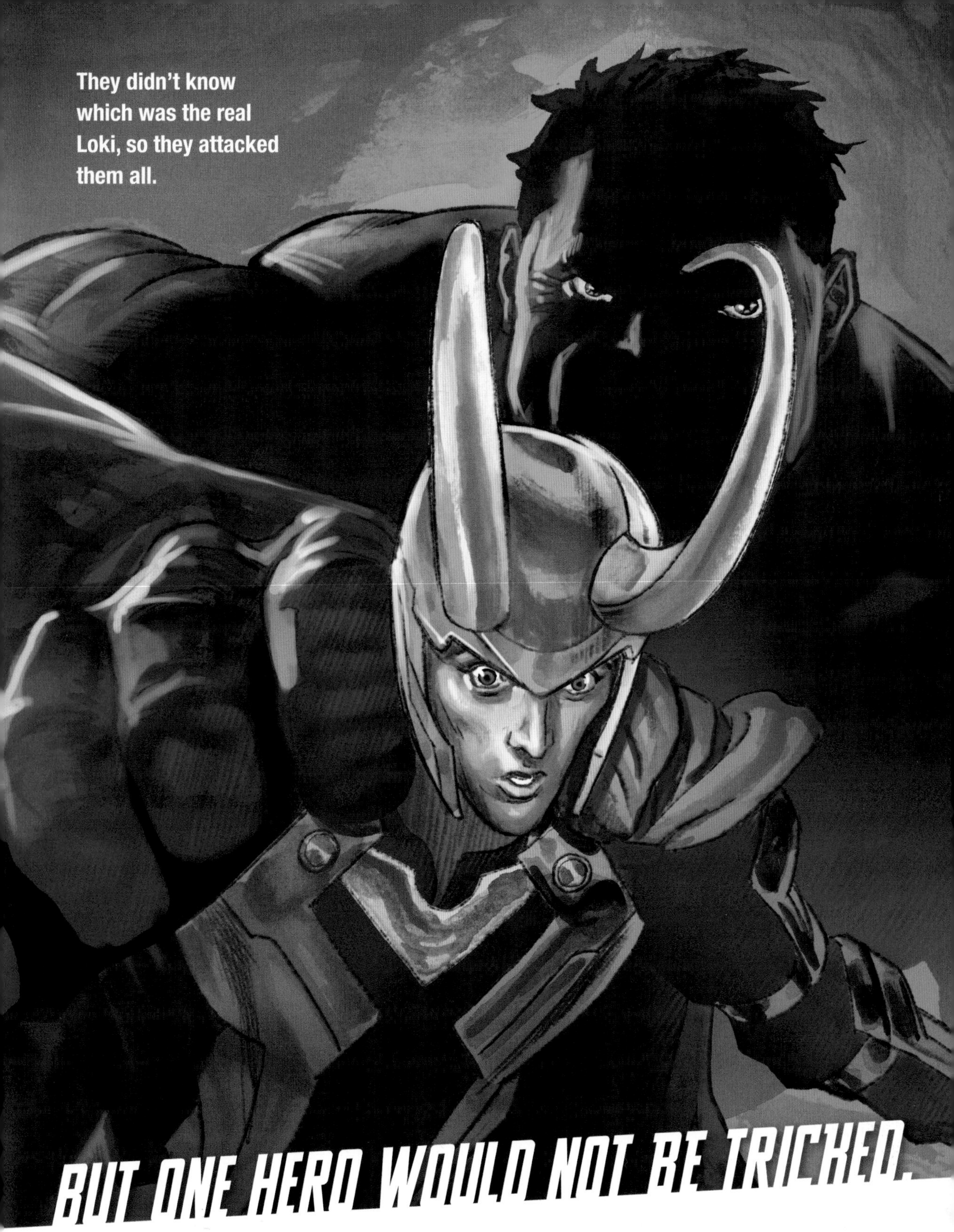
They didn't know which was the real Loki, so they attacked them all.
BUT ONE HERO WOULD NOT BE TRICKED.

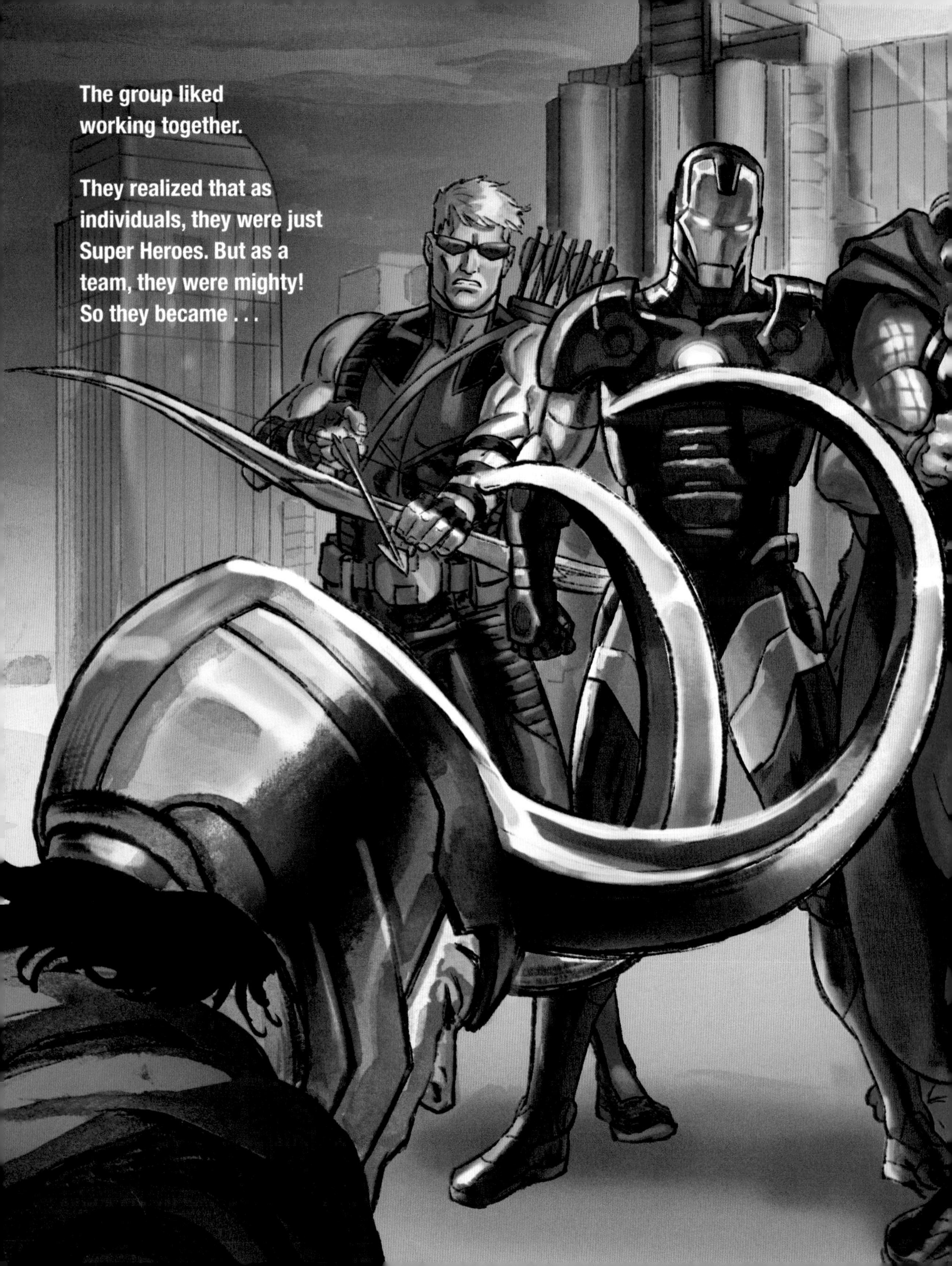

The group liked working together.

They realized that as individuals, they were just Super Heroes. But as a team, they were mighty! So they became . . .

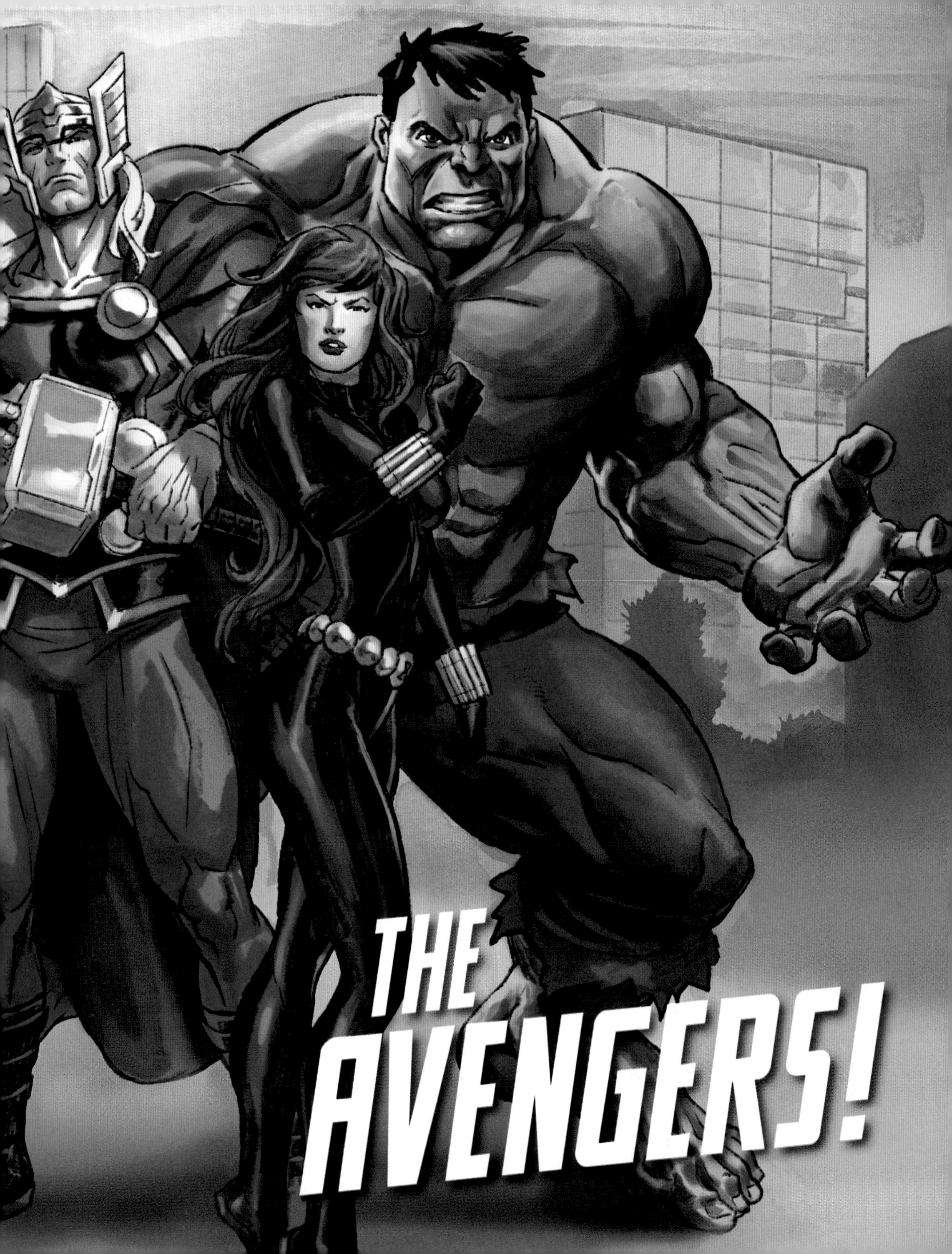
THE
AVENGERS!

HAWKEYE & BLACK WIDOW

returned to S.H.I.E.L.D.

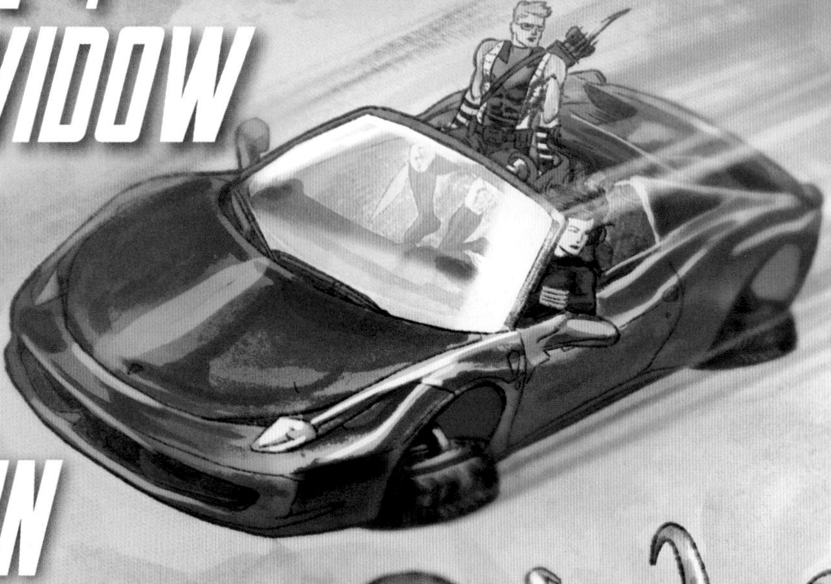

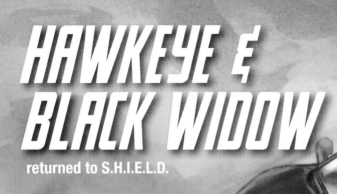

IRON MAN

went on with his life as the head of his company, Stark Industries.

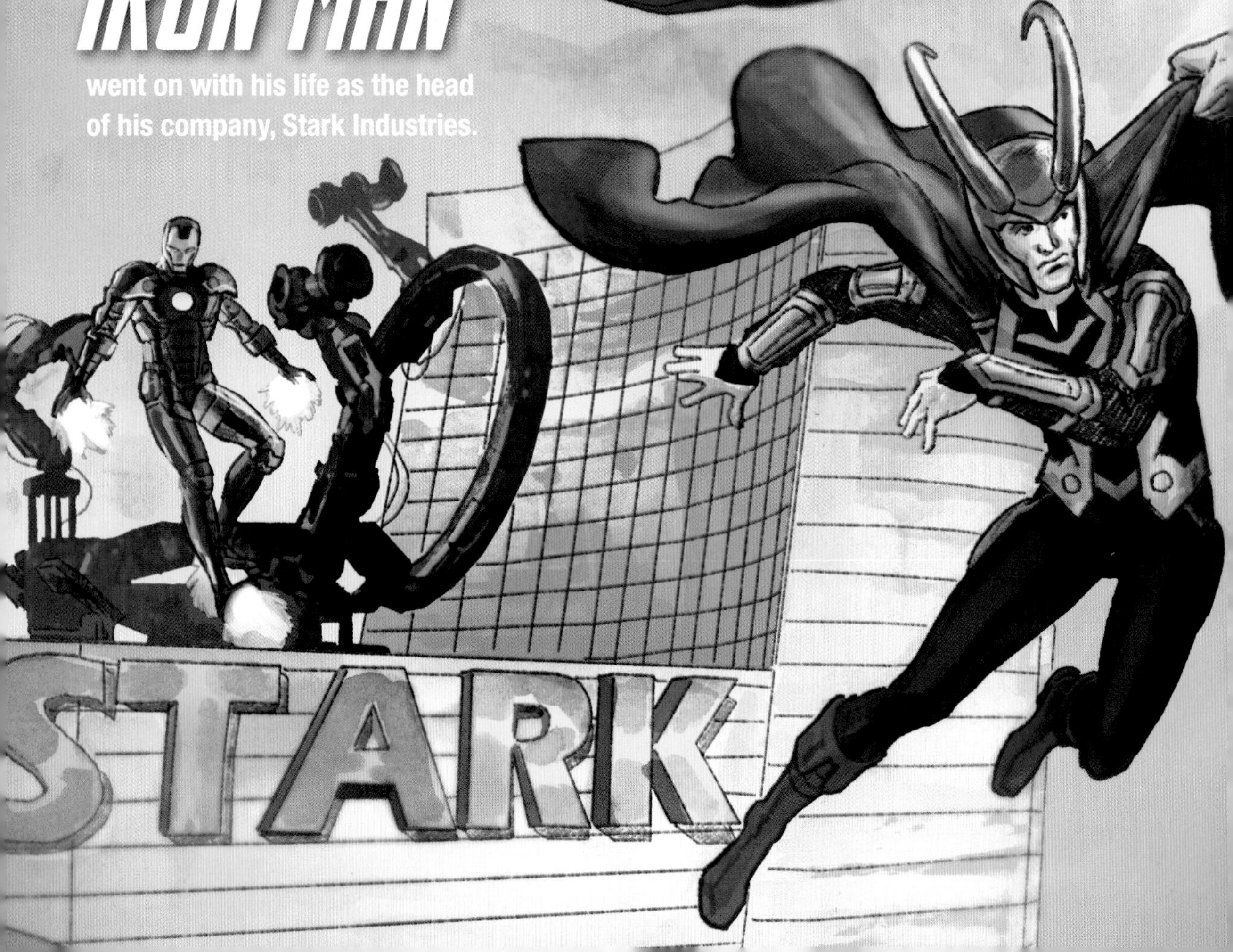

STARK

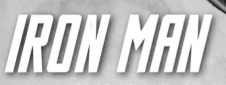

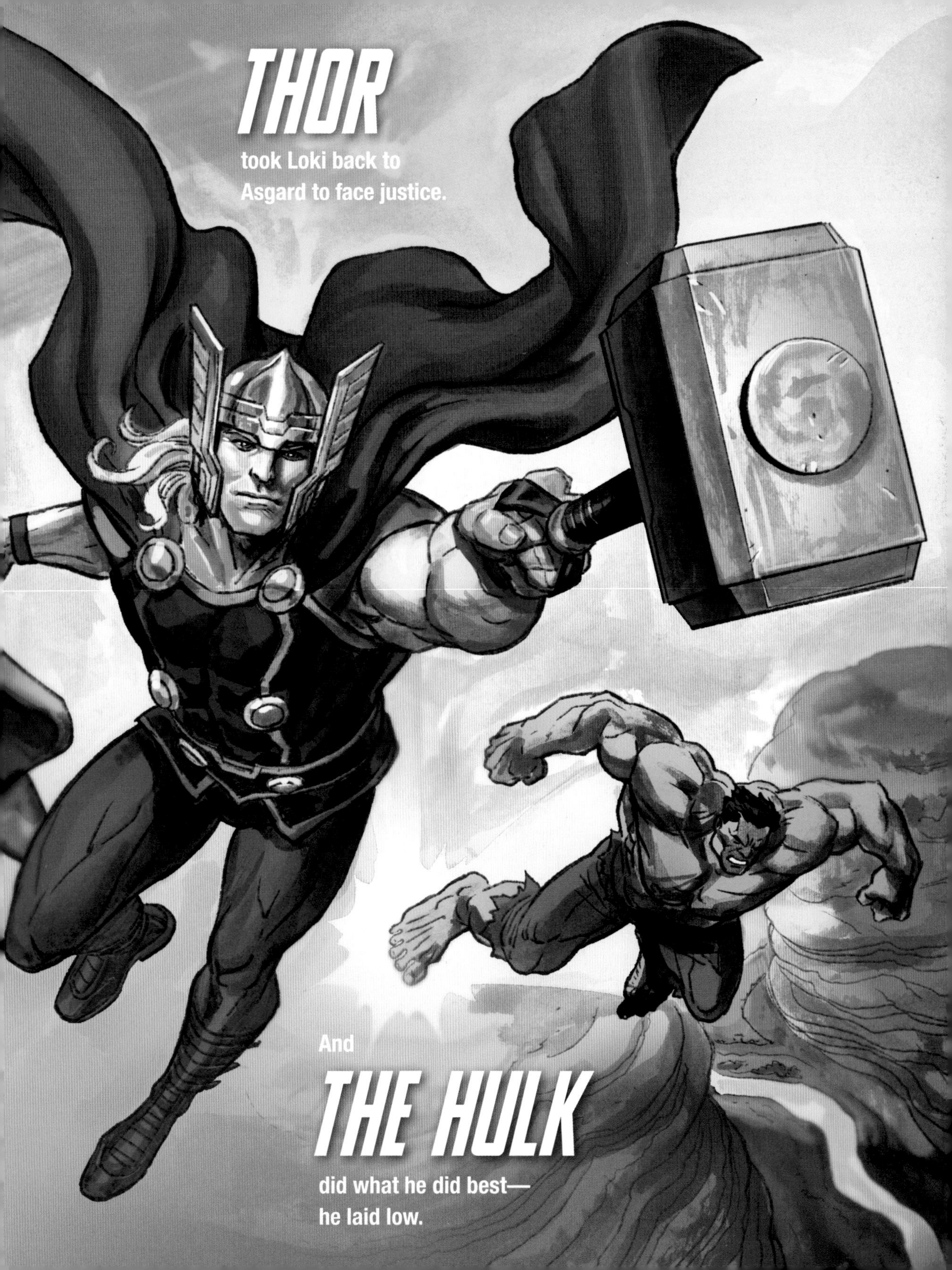

THOR

took Loki back to
Asgard to face justice.

And

THE HULK

did what he did best—
he laid low.

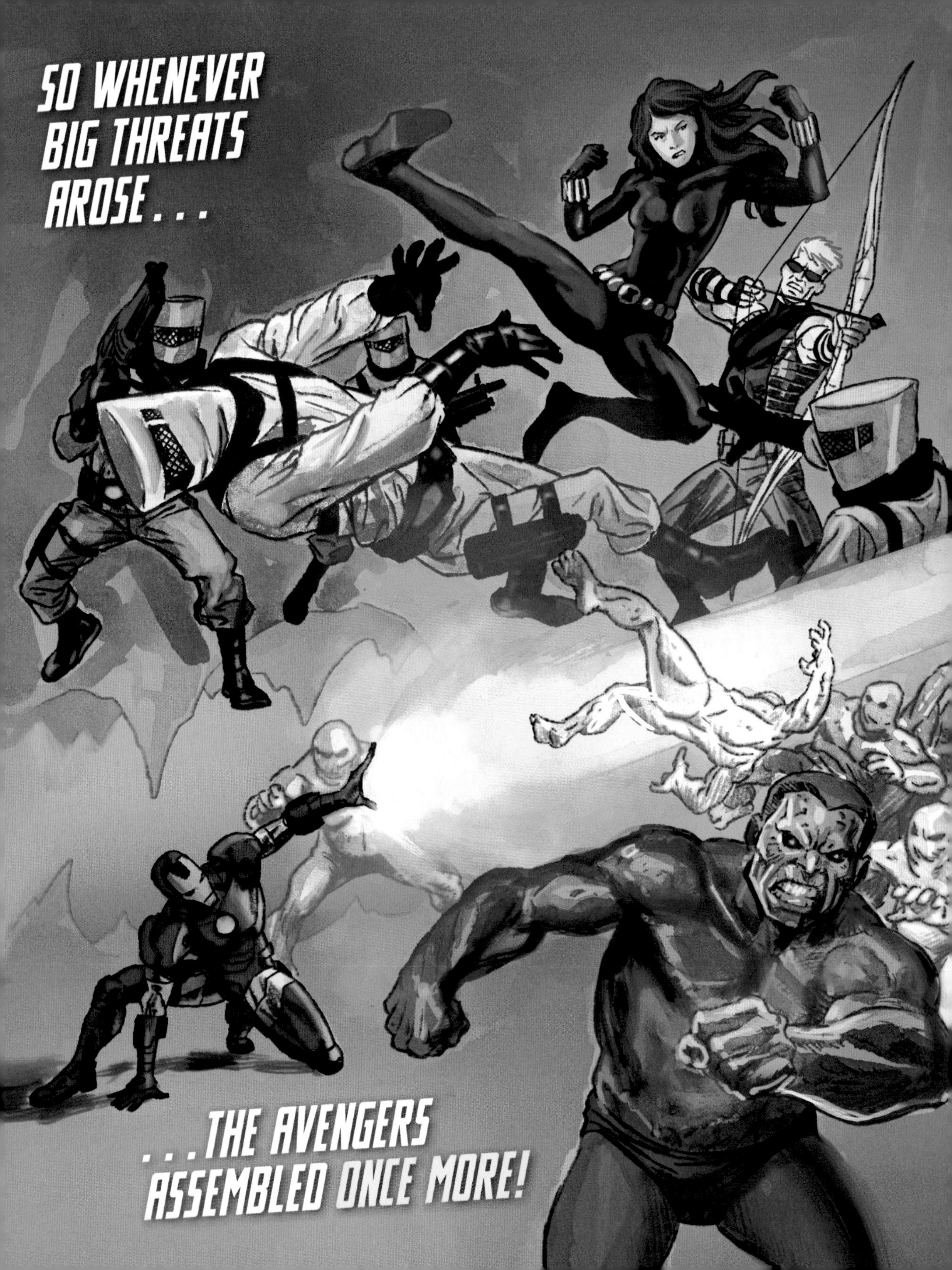
SO WHENEVER BIG THREATS AROSE . . .
. . .THE AVENGERS ASSEMBLED ONCE MORE!

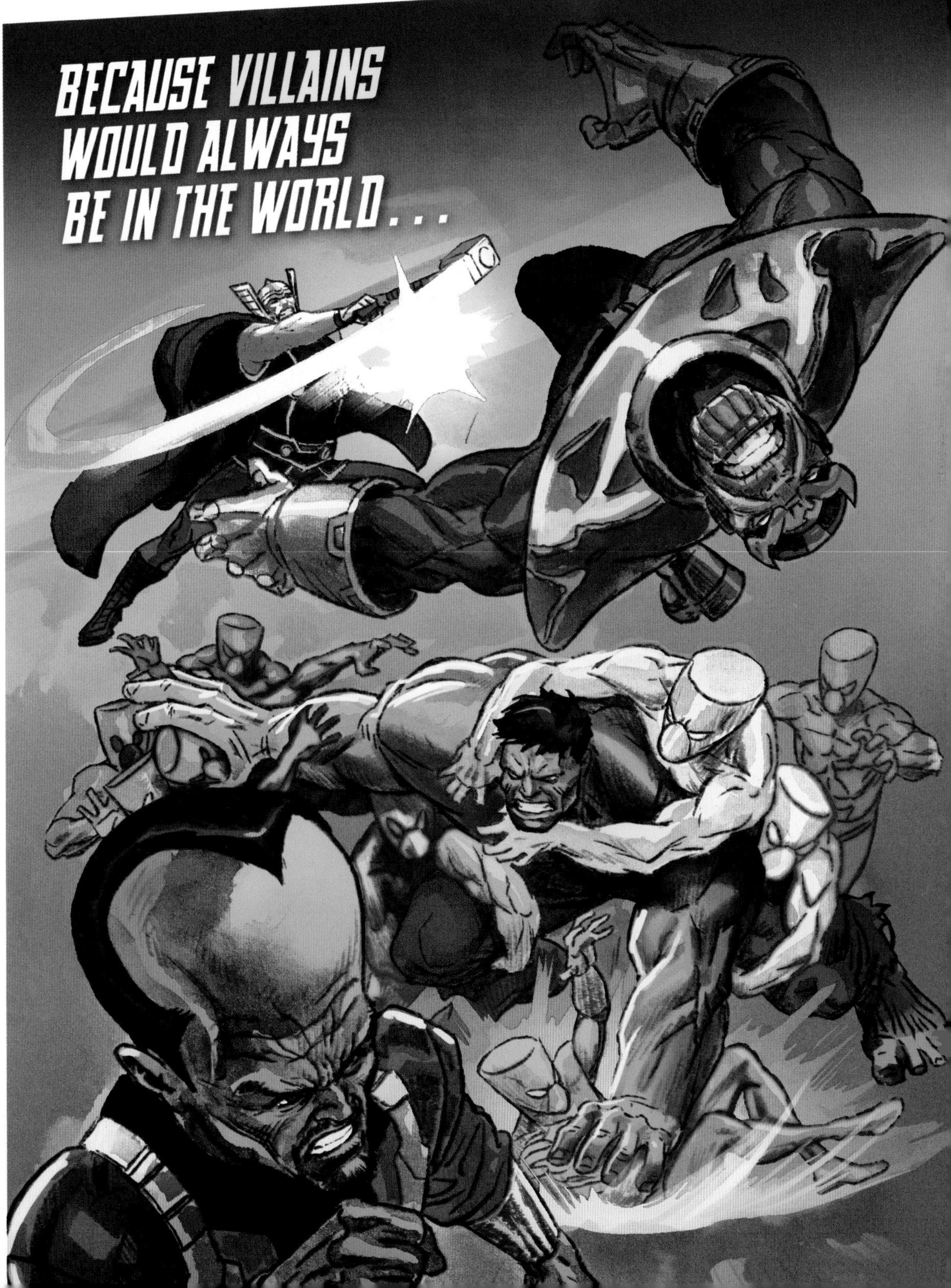

BECAUSE VILLAINS
WOULD ALWAYS
BE IN THE WORLD . . .

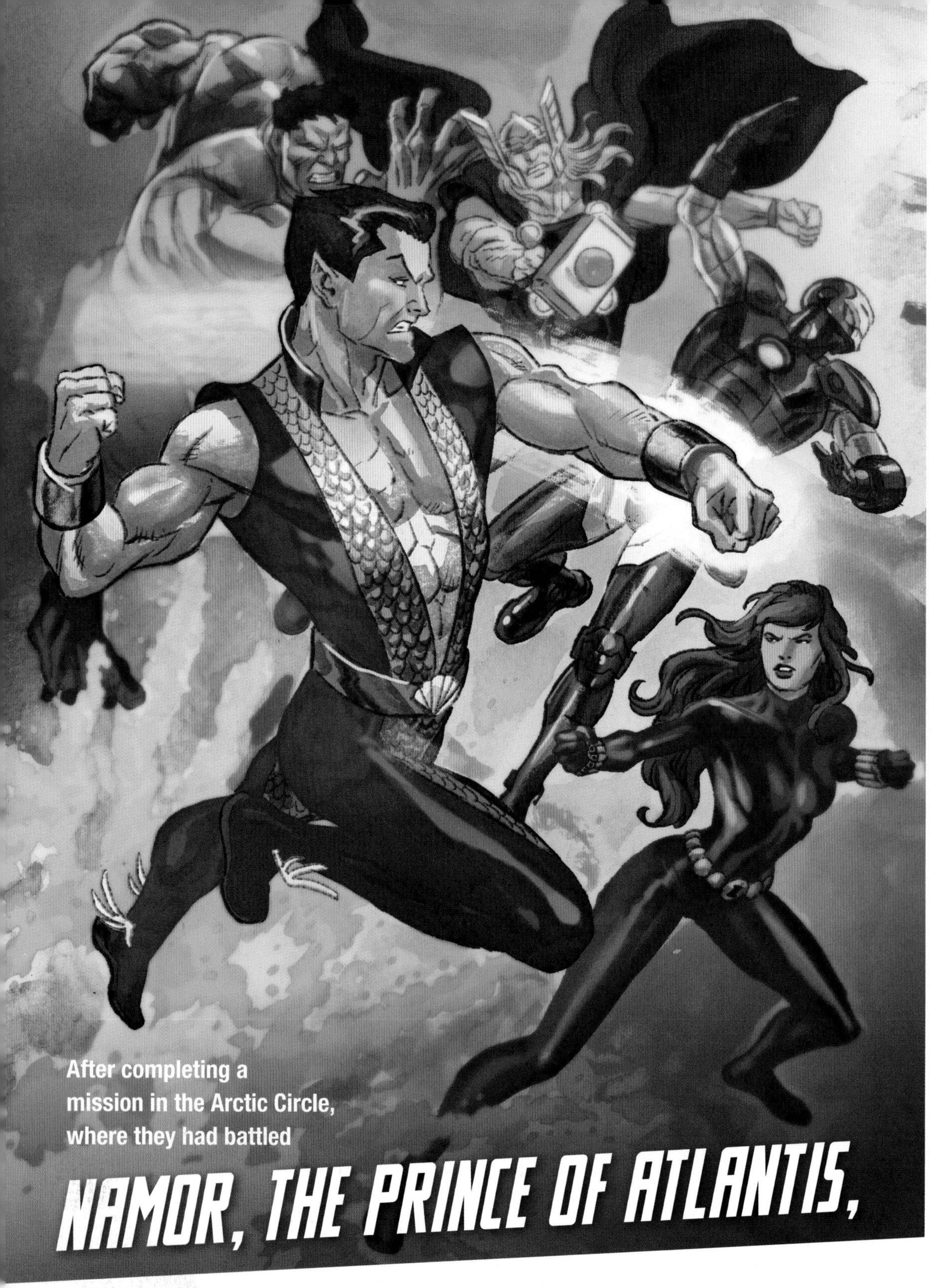

After completing a mission in the Arctic Circle, where they had battled

NAMOR, THE PRINCE OF ATLANTIS,

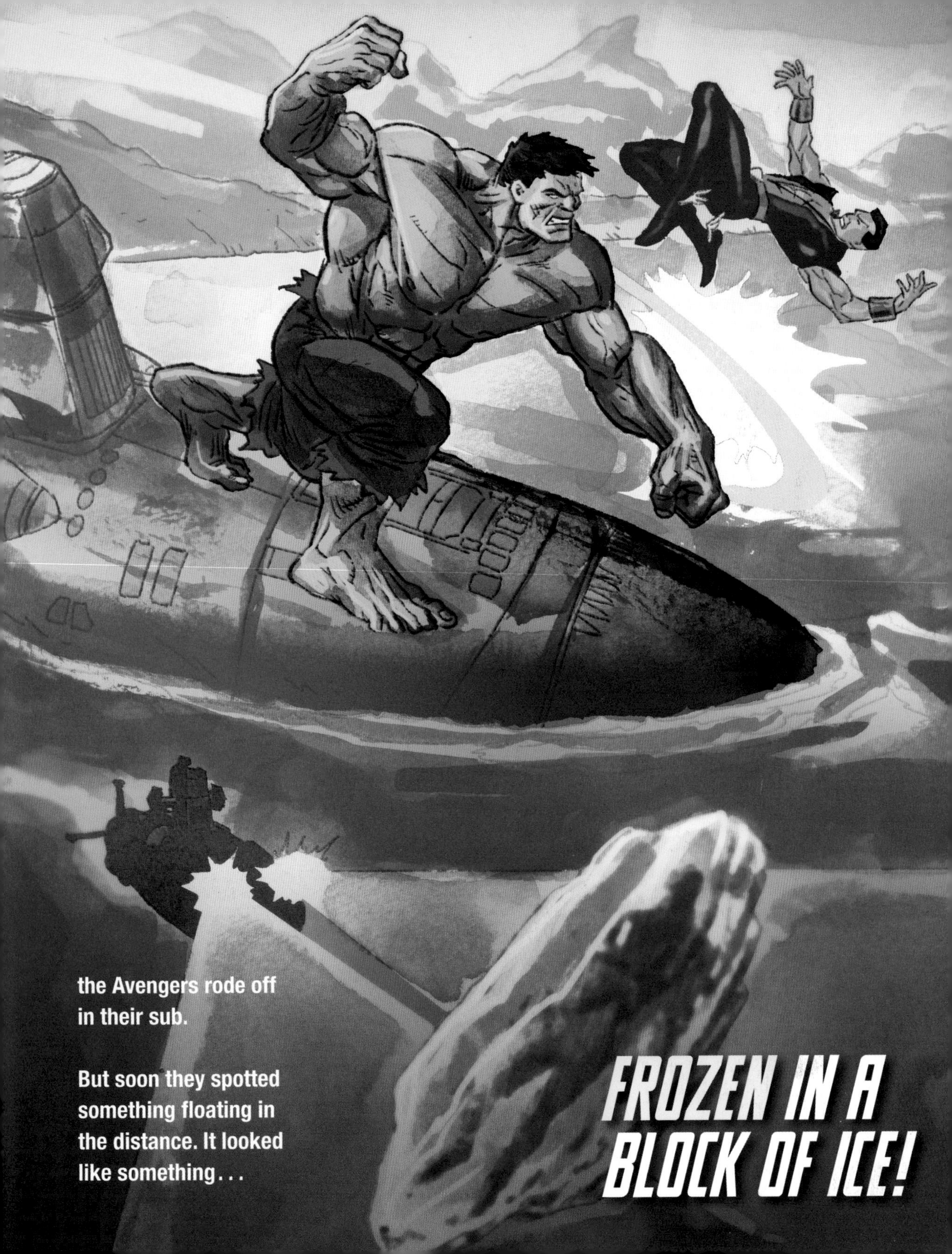

the Avengers rode off in their sub.

But soon they spotted something floating in the distance. It looked like something . . .

FROZEN IN A BLOCK OF ICE!

The Incredible Hulk swam to the figure and took it back to the sub. He took the block to the medical bay. There was a man trapped inside!

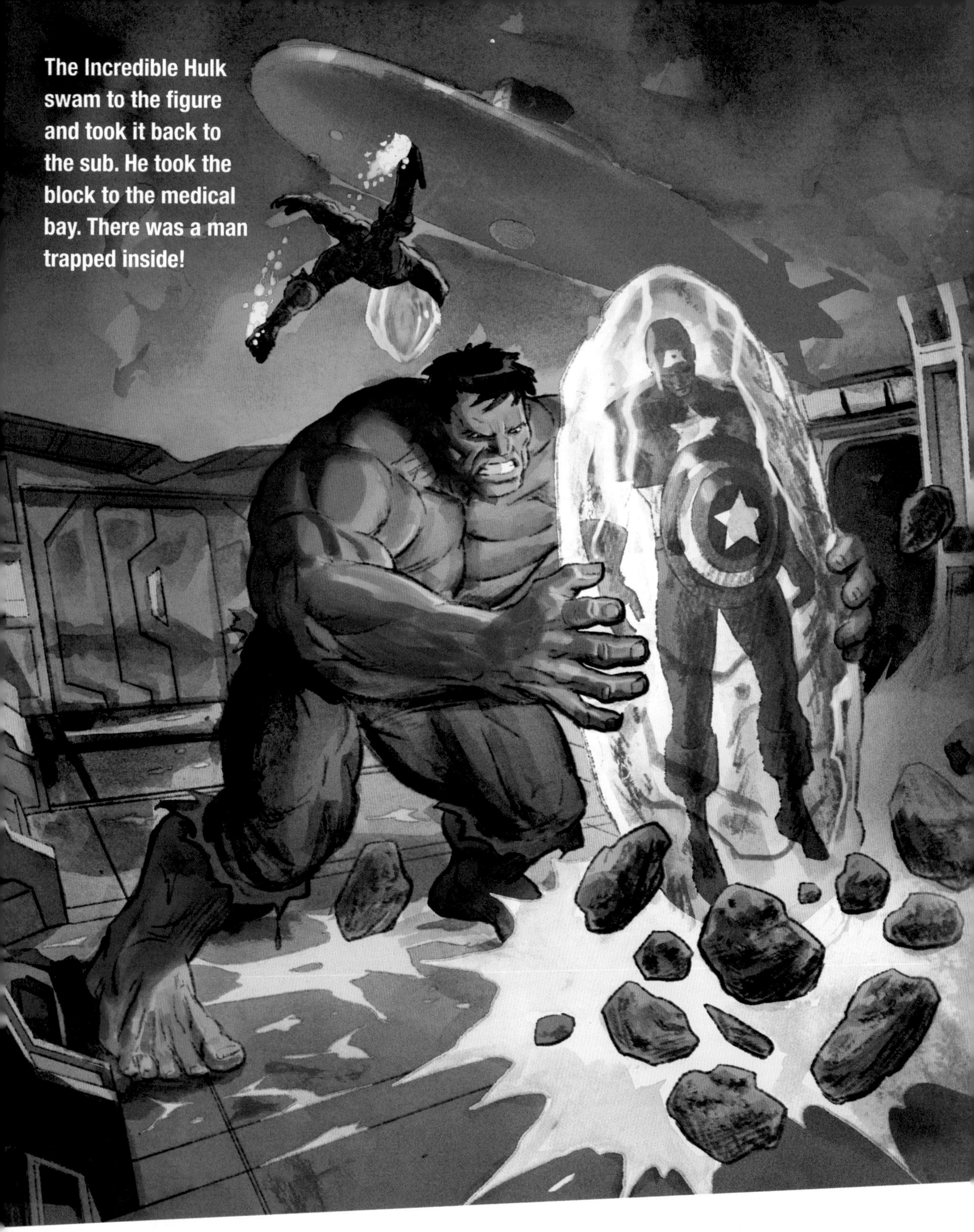

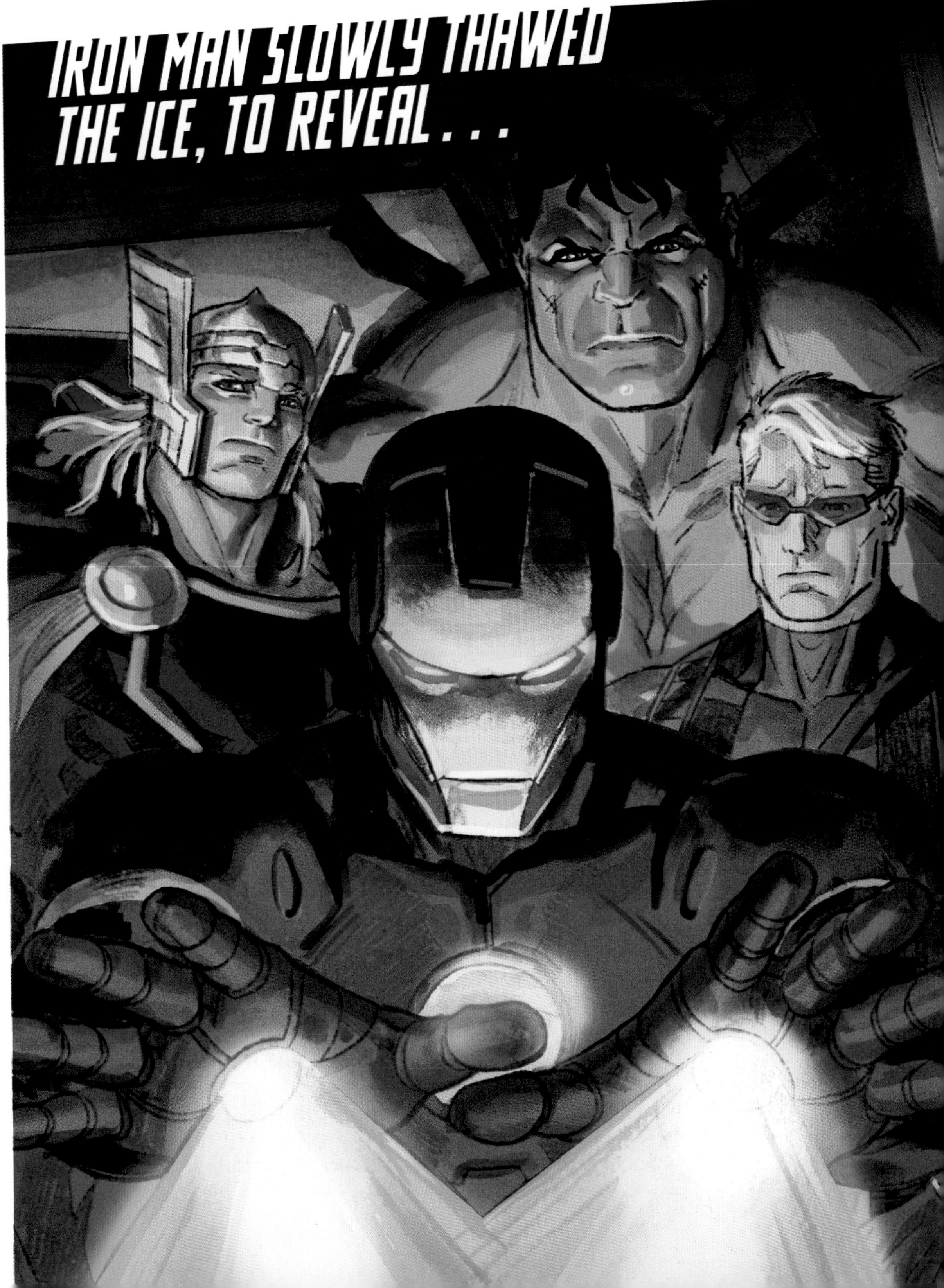
IRON MAN SLOWLY THAWED THE ICE, TO REVEAL . . .

CAPTAIN AMERICA,

THE FAMOUS HERO SUPER-SOLDIER FROM WORLD WAR II!

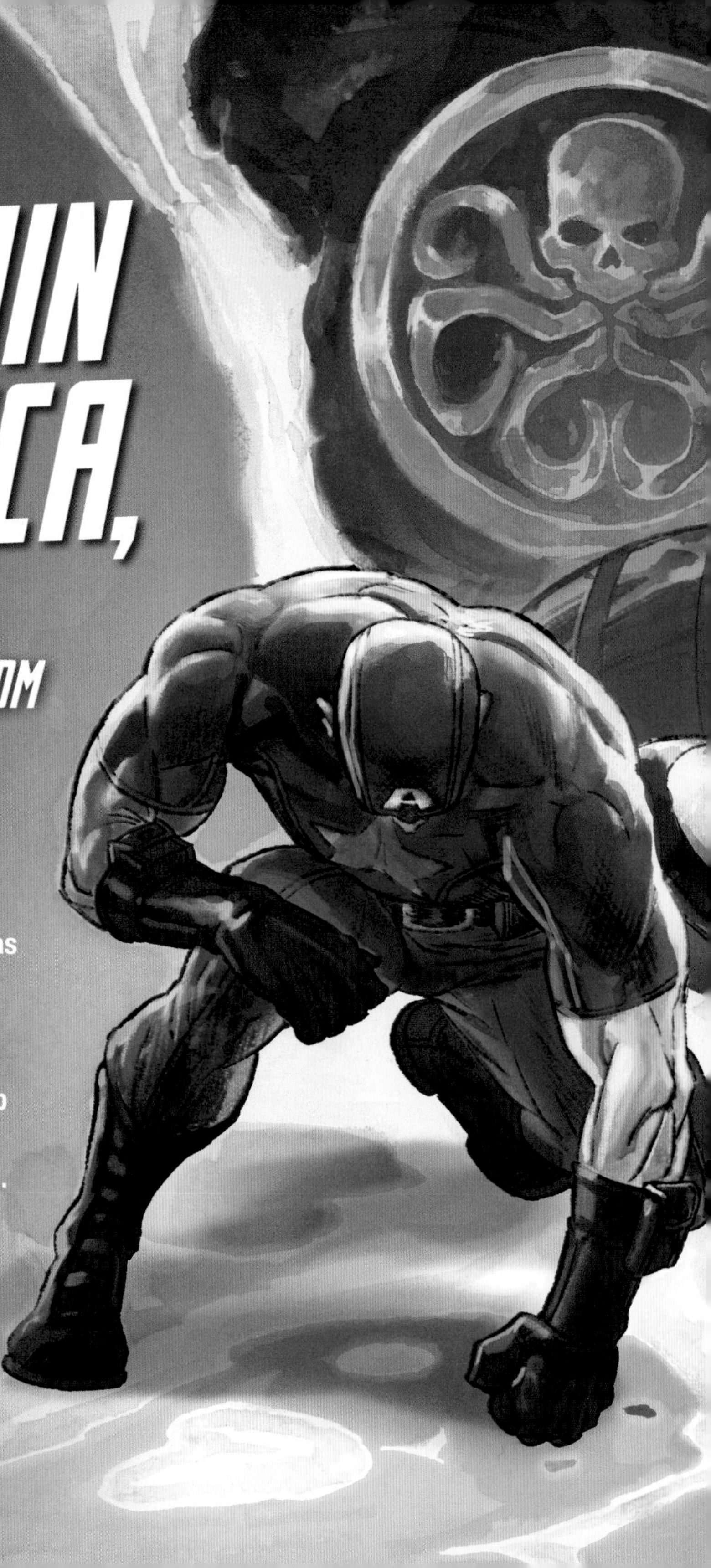

Cap saved America and the world from the evil organization Hydra and its leader, Red Skull. But he was trapped in ice and lay there for decades!

Confused and on guard, Cap listened to the Avengers explain what had happened. They told him they were friends.

But before the group could get too friendly, the sub shook.

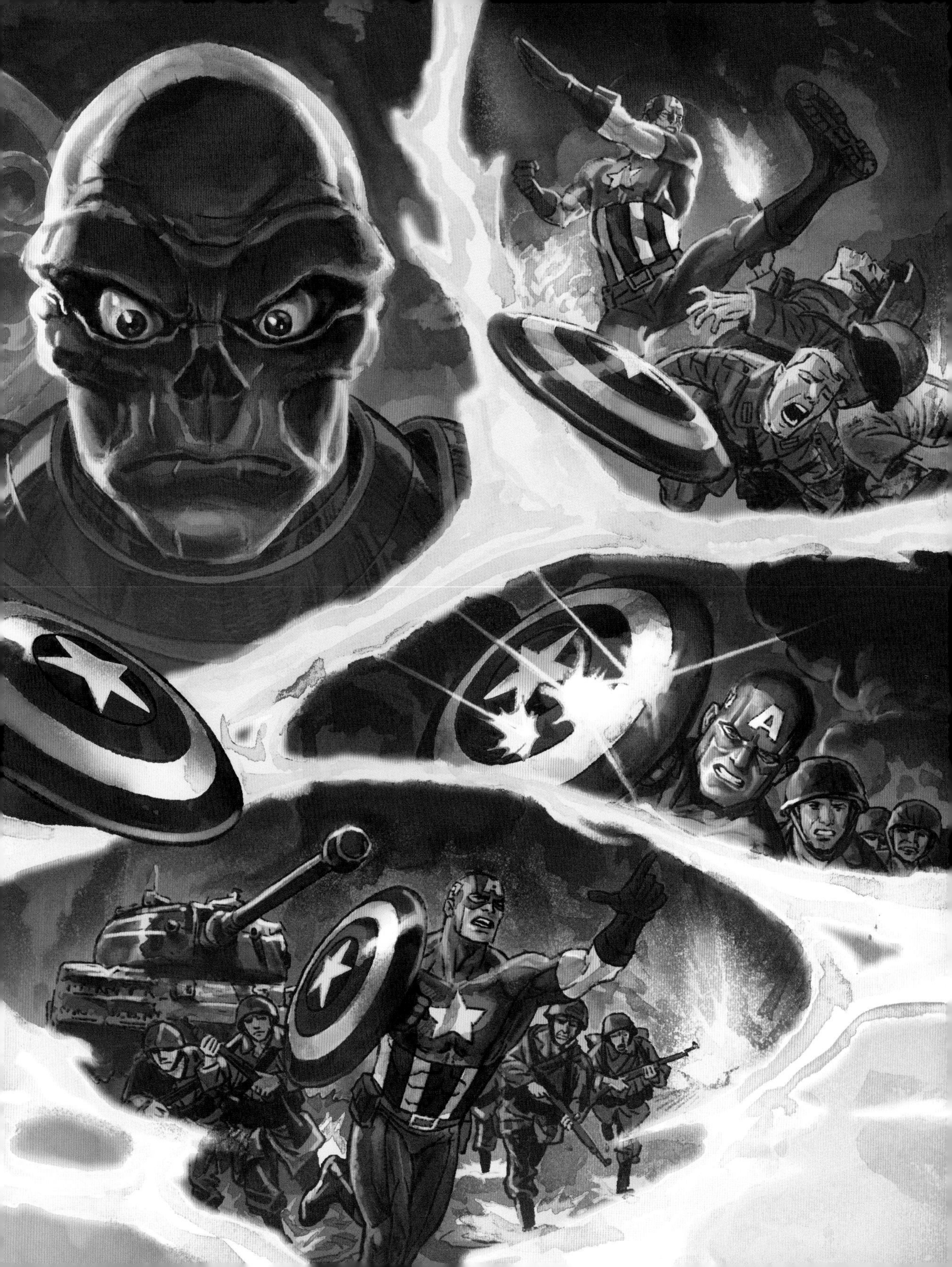

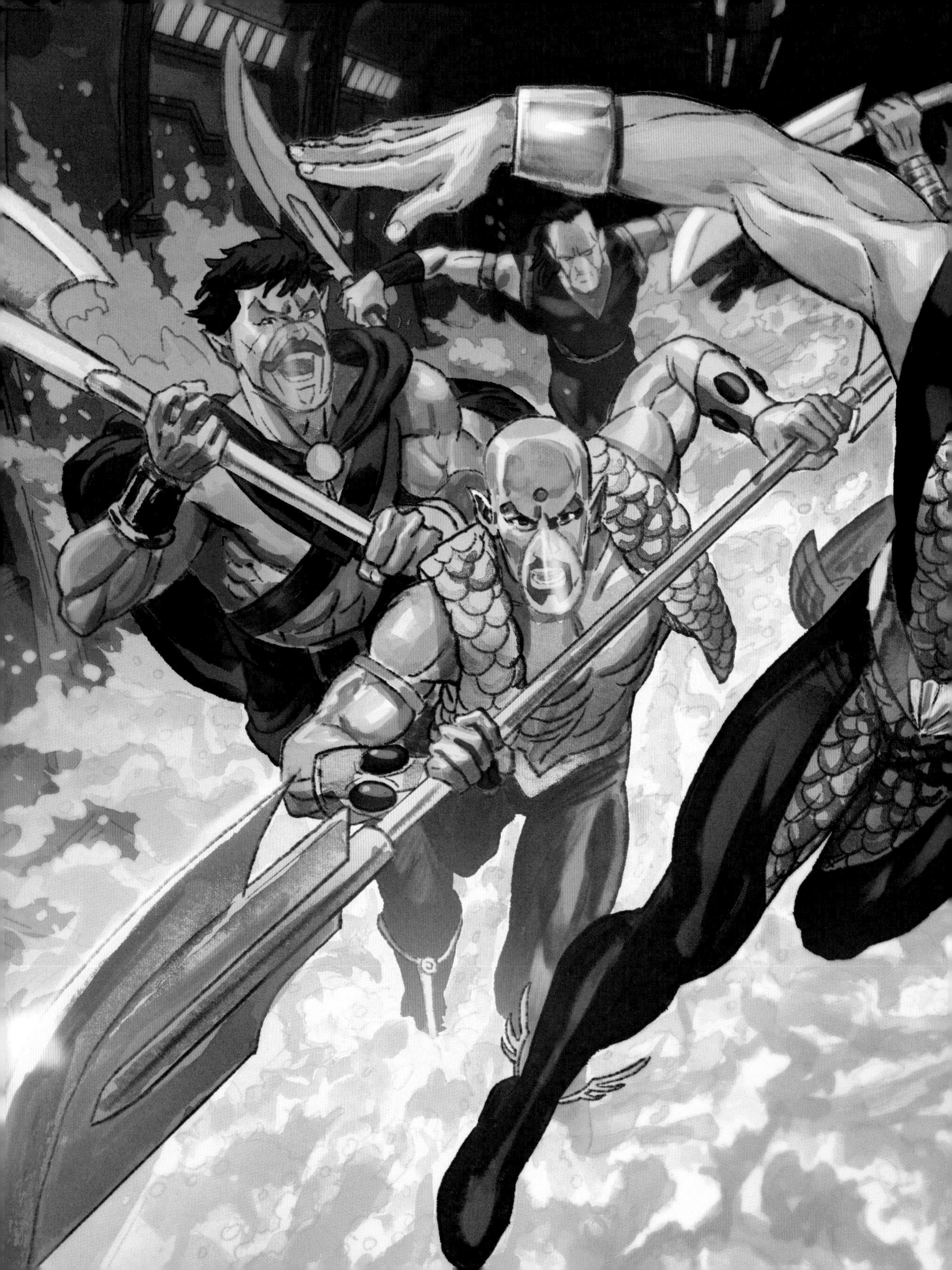

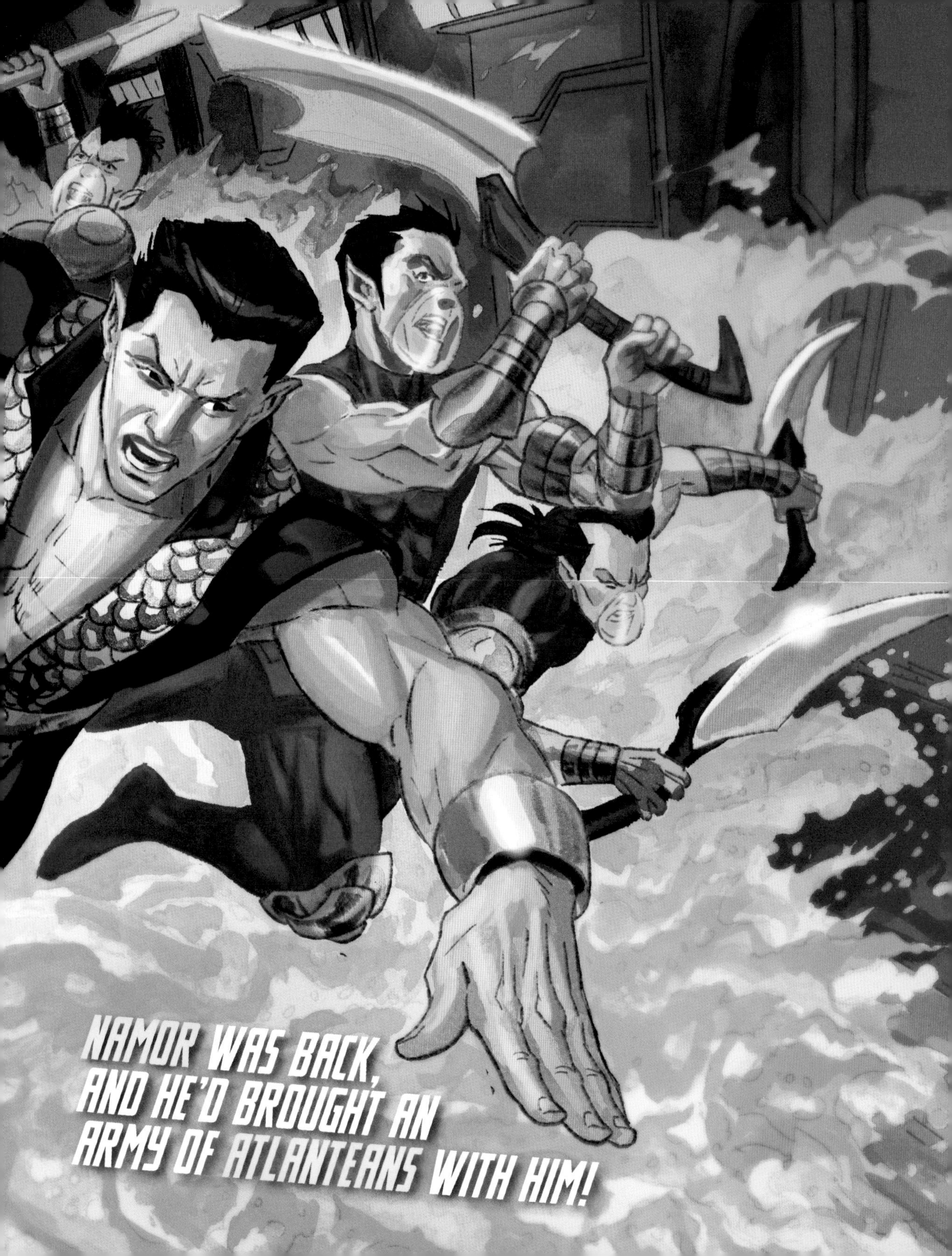
NAMOR WAS BACK, AND HE'D BROUGHT AN ARMY OF ATLANTEANS WITH HIM!

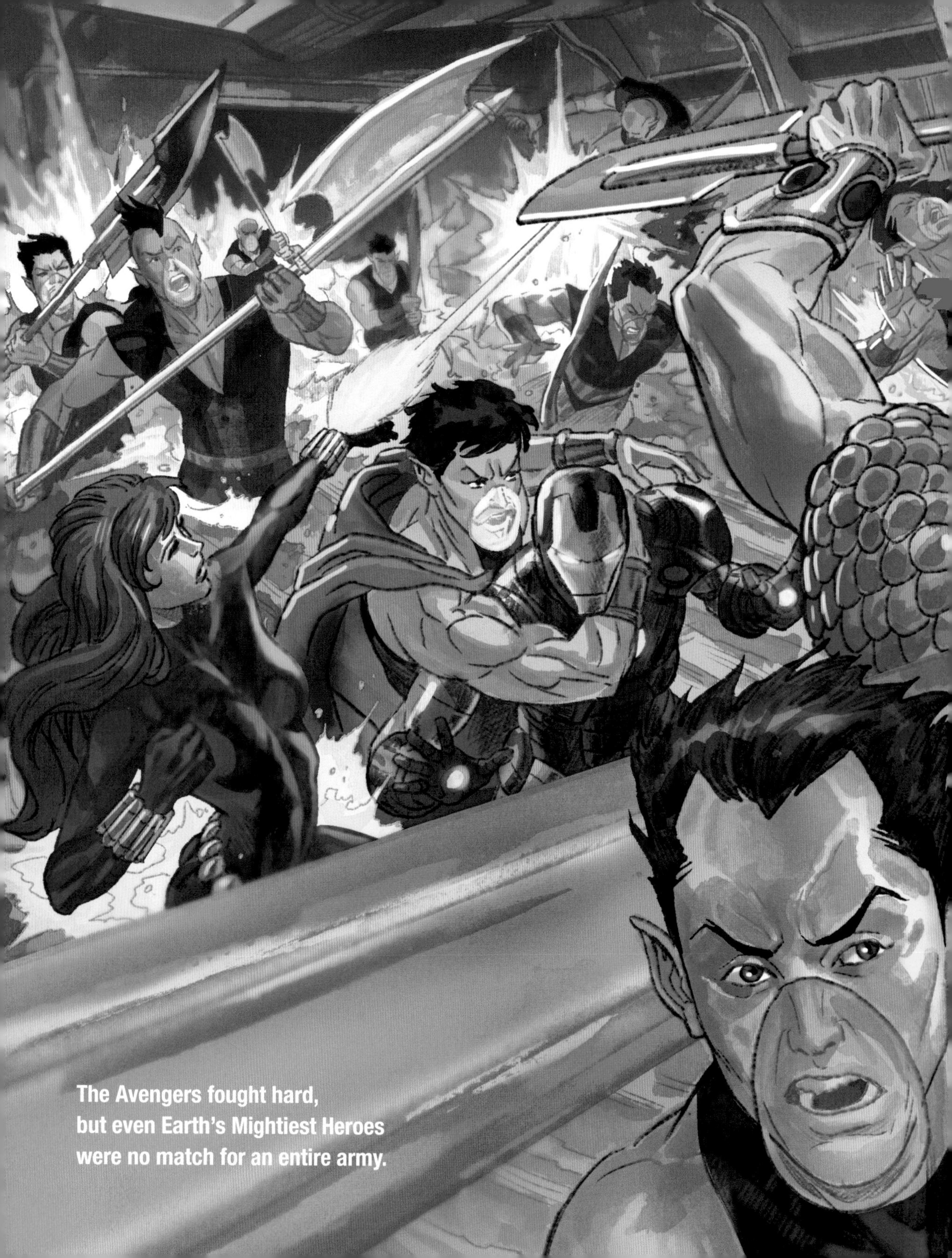

The Avengers fought hard,
but even Earth's Mightiest Heroes
were no match for an entire army.

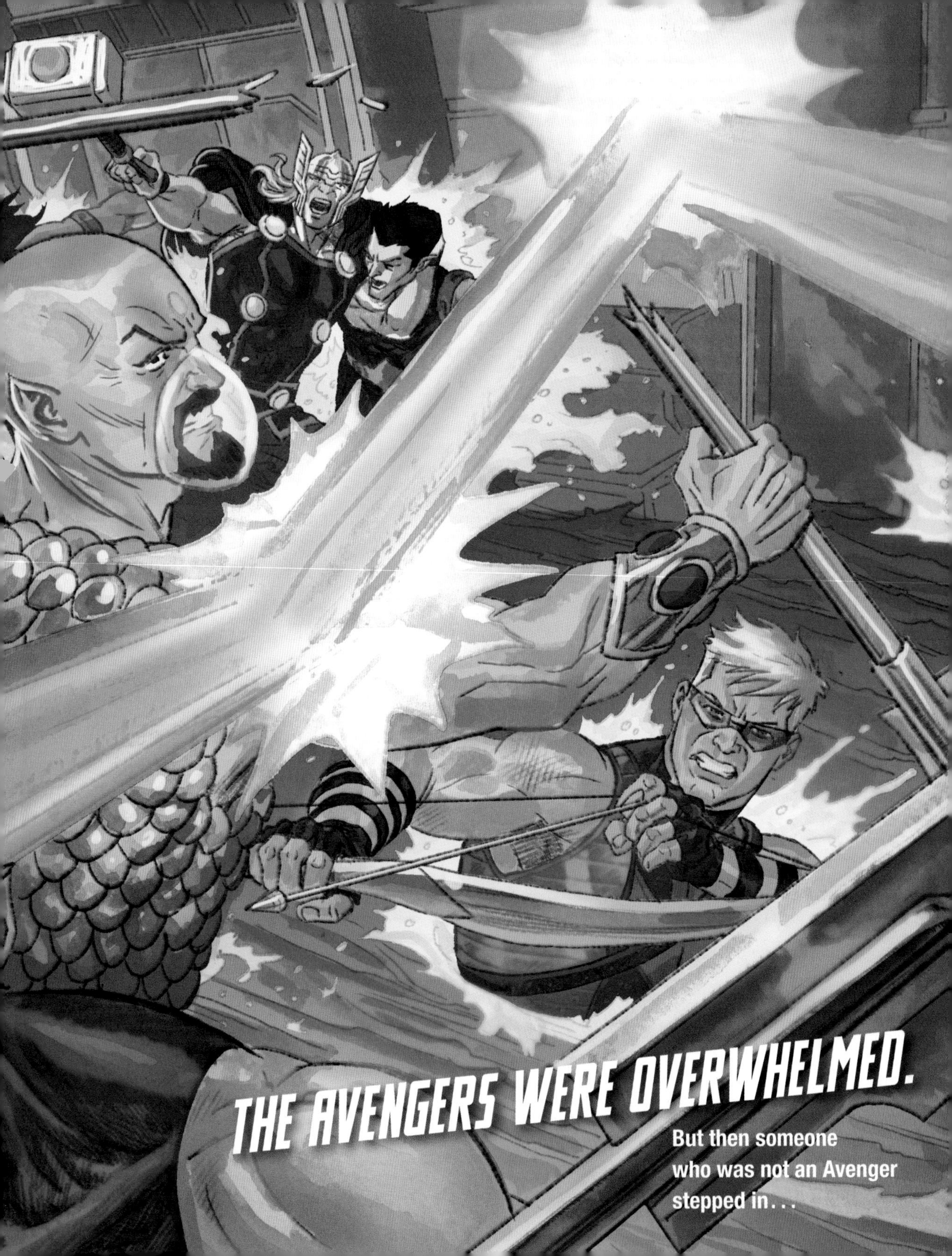

THE AVENGERS WERE OVERWHELMED.

But then someone
who was not an Avenger
stepped in. . .

. . . and the tide began to turn! The Avengers, together with Captain America, drove off Namor and his army. They had stopped him from waging war on the surface world.

They were proud of the way they had worked together. The final piece of their team was in place.

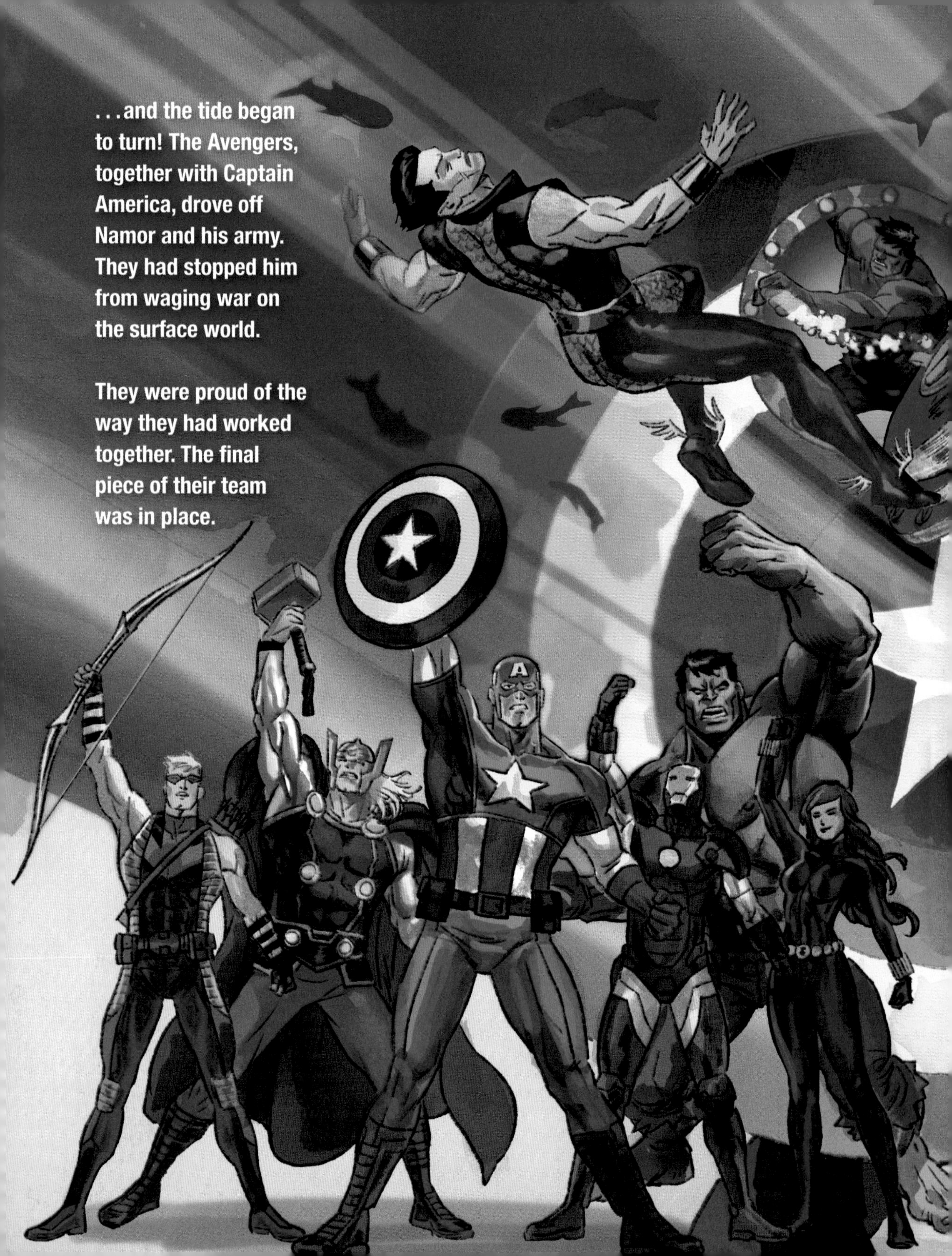